Aunt Alma gave them each a tall candle, and they climbed the stairs to their bedrooms. The thunder was closer now. It crashed loudly following an occasional zigzag of lightning. In the upstairs hall, the flickering candlelight caught the portrait Kelly had noticed earlier that day. Kelly stopped and studied the girl's face. A flash of lightning outside the window lit the hall briefly and in that instant, Kelly felt as if she were looking into a mirror. The girl in the portrait looked exactly like her.

Mystery of the Blue-Gowned Ghost

Linda Wirkner

The Colonial Williamsburg Foundation
Williamsburg, Virginia

Second printing, 1994

Cover art by Barbara Leonard Gibson

ISBN 0-87935-128-4

Printed in the United States of America

To John Capsis and Blossom Budney Tresselt

Chapter 1

The first thing Kelly Brennan noticed about Williamsburg, Virginia, was the intense heat. As soon as she stepped out of the air-conditioned bus, hot, sticky air wrapped around her like an unwanted wool blanket. Kelly set her suitcase down on the sizzling pavement. Next to it she placed her camera bag and tripod and the luggage carrier that held the boxes with her darkroom equipment. As she readjusted the cameras slung over each shoulder, her brother clumped down the bus steps. A skateboard was tucked under each arm and he was half-carrying, half-dragging a heavy suitcase that contained more books than clothes.

"Thanks for dropping us off here instead of at the station," Jared called to the bus driver. Jared pulled off his glasses and waved them around, trying to clear the steamed lenses. "Boy, Aunt Alma was right when she said Virginia summers were humid." A clump of light brown hair flopped onto his forehead and he reached up and brushed it back.

"I wonder where Aunt Alma is?" Kelly said. "She said she'd be here to meet us."

"You know Aunt Alma. Clocks and watches don't mean much to her. She always loses track of time." When Jared reached into the pocket on the side of his suitcase for the Colonial Williamsburg guidebook their aunt had sent them, Kelly braced herself.

"That's the College of William and Mary at the end of the street," Jared said, "and the Capitol is at the other end." Jared paused and looked at Kelly with a mischievous twinkle in his eye. "Did you know that Duke of Gloucester Street was named after Prince William, duke of Gloucester, the eldest surviving son of Queen Anne, and that this street is nearly a mile long and ninety-nine feet wide?"

Kelly clamped her hands over her ears. "Don't start, Jared Brennan. I don't intend to spend my summer listening to you spout what you consider to be fascinating facts."

Jared grinned and shrugged his shoulders. "I just thought you'd be interested. After all, Dad does expect you to learn some history this summer."

Kelly decided to ignore Jared's teasing. Her mother was always telling her that Jared only teased her because she reacted so strongly. Maybe her mother was right. "I think I'll take a few pictures while we're waiting," she said.

They were standing on the corner of Henry Street and Duke of Gloucester Street, just on the edge of the Historic Area of Colonial Williamsburg. Duke of Gloucester Street was closed to traffic during the day, and this morning the street bustled with hundreds of tourists. Some strolled beneath the shade of elm or maple trees. Others hurried along, pointing out various sights to their companions. Small children, wearing souvenir black felt, three-cornered hats or white mobcaps, trailed after their parents. Kelly's lively green eyes took in the scene eagerly.

Toward the college end of town, Merchants Square housed dozens of shops in old-fashioned colonial buildings. Outside restaurants, white and black wrought-iron tables and chairs were arranged among wooden planters filled with bright red and yellow petunias. A canopy of spreading crape myrtle trees covered the brick sidewalk.

Looking down the wide street in the opposite direction, Kelly saw green and gold and red carriages pulled by shining black horses. What fun it would be to ride in one of those, she thought. Colonial homes and shops, some fronted by white picket fences or unpainted plank fences, lined the street for as far as she could see. Outside the buildings, men and women dressed in colonial costumes stood talking to visitors.

Near the end of the block she saw a young woman wearing a pale yellow, flowered, ankle-length gown with a wide neckline and elbow-length sleeves trimmed with stiff white ruffles. On her head she wore a white cap edged with lace. Forgetting for the moment that she didn't care about history, Kelly peered through her camera and adjusted the lens for a sharp focus. This was going to be a great place to take pictures, she thought excitedly. She snapped the shutter and advanced the film, ready for another shot.

Above the doorway of a small white building hung a strange picture sign, and Kelly zoomed in for a closer look. She saw a man standing in front of the building studying what looked like a guide map. Through her zoom lens, Kelly saw that his face was tanned and leathery, as if he spent a lot of time out-doors. His dark, bushy hair stuck out as if blown by a strong wind, although the heavy air was still. The man's stocky, stoop-shouldered body and slightly bent back reminded Kelly of a giant peanut. He looked up from his map just as Kelly snapped the picture.

Much to her surprise, the peanut-shaped man

charged across the street toward her. "What do you think you're doing?" he growled. "Why did you take my picture?"

"I . . . I was just photographing the buildings," Kelly stammered.

The man glared at her for a moment, then turned abruptly and headed down the street.

"What was that all about?" Jared asked. But before Kelly could explain, a plump, gray-haired woman wearing a gaily colored blue- and yellow-flowered blouse hurried toward them. Her violet eyes were shining and her squarish face was flushed. She threw her arms around Kelly and Jared in a warm embrace.

"I know I'm late," Alma Maxwell said breathlessly. "I was busy sorting through things for a yard sale and I lost track of time." Kelly and Jared looked at each other and grinned. "Welcome to Colonial Williamsburg," their aunt said with a bright smile that turned to a look of dismay when her glance dropped to their assortment of belongings heaped on the sidewalk. "Oh, my. Are *all* those things yours?"

Kelly nodded her curly brown head. "We thought we should only bring what we absolutely needed for the summer."

"Yes, I see," Aunt Alma said dubiously. "I'm

not sure exactly how we're going to carry all this back to the house. It's nearly three blocks from here, you know." She looked around in obvious confusion.

"I'm sure we can manage, Aunt Alma," Kelly said quickly. She began scooping up bags and camera equipment.

Suddenly, Aunt Alma looked relieved. "Chen," she called across the street. "Could you come here, please?"

Aunt Alma was waving to a boy who looked about Kelly's age. He had thick, straight hair the color of ink. His bronze skin was a golden shade that Kelly thought would make the perfect tan if she didn't always burn so easily. As he crossed the street toward them, he smiled and his dark eyes seem to disappear. "Hi, Miss Maxwell," the boy said. "What's the problem?"

Aunt Alma pointed to the pile of luggage and other items on the sidewalk, then introduced Chen to Kelly and Jared. As soon as everyone had gathered up as much as possible, Aunt Alma led the way down the side street.

As they walked, Chen said to the young Brennans, "Your aunt told me you were coming to spend the summer. I live across the street from her."

"Actually, Aunt Alma is our mother's aunt. I guess that makes her our great-aunt. Our parents are teaching in an exchange program in England this summer," Kelly explained. "Aunt Alma invited us to stay with her while they're away."

"You'll like it here. There's lots to do and see." To Jared, Chen said, "I see you're into skateboards, too."

"Hey, do you have one?" Jared asked.

"I sure do. Just got some new trucks for it."

Kelly only half-listened to the talk of trucks and wheels. After walking only two blocks, beads of perspiration stood out on her forehead and upper lip and her blue cotton blouse stuck to her back as if it were glued in place.

"You'll get used to the humidity after a while," Aunt Alma told her when she noticed Kelly attempting to blow wisps of damp hair from her forehead. "We're almost there. I hope you and Jared will be comfortable in such an old, run-down place. I've only been in it a few months since I inherited it from my uncle. I'm afraid it's been rather neglected for a number of years."

"Oh, I won't mind," Kelly assured her. "I like old houses."

Aunt Alma frowned slightly as she continued almost to herself, "It's not just that the house is so

13

run-down. It's just that . . . I hope everything will be OK." Kelly looked quizzically at her aunt. Had she changed her mind about wanting them to spend the summer? Or was something else bothering her?

Before Kelly could ask any questions, Aunt Alma stopped in front of a large, peculiar-looking house that sprawled in several directions as if parts had been added over the years without following any clear design. A front porch ran the length of the center brick section. Many of the posts on the porch railing were either sagging or missing entirely. Twin chimneys rose above the roofline at each end of the brick portion.

Wood-framed wings had been added to either side of this main building. At the end of the left wing stood a fat, round wooden tower that was pointed at the top like a witch's hat.

The shutters on several of the windows were loose, and the white paint on the wood sections was chipped and peeling. The yard was also in need of some attention. Overgrown holly tangled with nearby boxwood shrubs. Tall tufts of grass peeked up through a thick mat of leaves dropped by huge magnolia trees that surrounded the house.

Kelly supposed the house had been quite elegant long ago, but now, as Aunt Alma opened the front door, Kelly leaned over and whispered to

Jared, "It looks like a haunted house."

Jared rolled his eyes at his sister in response. But Aunt Alma turned toward them with a frightened look and asked, "Why would you say that?"

Chapter 2

Kelly stared at her aunt. But there was no chance to ask questions, for Aunt Alma quickly went into the house. Kelly stepped through the doorway and set the heavy suitcase and camera bag down on the floor of the wide front hall. After the glaring sunlight, she had to blink in order to adjust to the dimly lit wood-paneled hall. After a moment, she was able to see a wide walnut staircase to the left. Halfway up there was a small, square landing lit by an oval window before the stairs made a sharp turn and continued up to the second floor.

"The living room is this way," Aunt Alma told them, pointing to a double doorway to the right. "It's a bit of a mess right now," she added. "I'm using it to organize things I hope to sell in the yard sale."

Kelly saw little evidence of organization. Lamps, small brass candy dishes, end tables, and a wild assortment of miscellaneous items cluttered every corner of the room. Cardboard boxes over-flowing with knickknacks and dishes were squeezed between old, battered-looking chairs with torn and faded upholstery.

"We could help you sort through these things, Aunt Alma. Jared and I have helped Mom with lots of yard sales."

"That's right," Jared agreed. "Mom whirls through the house with a vengeance every spring. She says a yearly yard sale is the only way to keep from being overrun with junk."

Kelly laughed and added, "It's kind of fun. It's amazing what kinds of odds and ends people will buy."

Aunt Alma nervously ran a dimpled hand through her wavy gray hair. "Well, I hope this sale makes enough to pay for some of the repairs this house needs. And I'd really appreciate your help." She gestured vaguely toward the clutter. "I really have no idea how much money I can raise. It may not be enough to keep the house. Especially now that . . . " Her voice trailed off and she seemed lost in her thoughts.

"Miss Maxwell?" Chen said softly.

Aunt Alma jumped slightly. Chen said if she didn't need any more help, he should be getting home to mow the lawn. "But maybe I could take

Kelly and Jared over to the Historic Area after lunch," he added. "There's going to be a militia muster in front of the Magazine."

After Chen left, Aunt Alma took Kelly and Jared up to their bedrooms. "Why don't you two have a look around the house while I go downstairs and make some sandwiches for lunch?"

Kelly's room was at the end of a long, narrow hall that ran the length of the right wing of the house. She looked around the bedroom happily. Compared to her tiny one back home, this room was huge. There was a maple wood four-poster bed with a matching dresser. In one corner, a large overstuffed chair covered with faded green and yellow fabric had a matching footstool. In the opposite corner stood an oval table made from a darker wood than the bed and dresser. Chairs with tall backs had been arranged at either end of the table.

The wallpaper background had probably been white once, but now it was dirtied and gray. Splashed across it was a pattern of huge yellow sunflowers and dark green leaves in various shapes and sizes. Kelly wasn't crazy about the wallpaper, but she loved the high double windows that opened outward in a semicircle. The window seat covered with a plump green cushion would be a great place in which to curl up with a book.

18

Kelly decided to unpack later and left her room to explore the rest of the upstairs. Another bedroom across the hall, painted a dark blue, was filled with heavy pieces of oak furniture. The room was gloomy, and Kelly shivered as she pulled the door closed and continued down the hall. She followed the turn in the corridor and came out into a slightly wider hall. A soft, scuffling sound came from a room to her right, and, thinking it was probably Jared, she opened double doors to it. "Jared," she called.

There was no answer. Kelly stood in the doorway, listening, but heard nothing more. This room appeared to be a study dominated by an enormous dark wood desk and floor-to-ceiling bookcases that lined one entire wall. Jared will love all those books, she thought as she closed the door behind her and tiptoed back down the hall. She wasn't sure why she was tiptoeing, but something about these dark, shadowy hallways gave her a weird, shivery feeling, as if she shouldn't disturb anything.

Coming back to the wide central passage, she was attracted by a portrait of a young girl hanging on the wall near the stairs. Kelly thought the girl must have been about her age or a little older when the portrait was painted. The girl had dark brown hair that hung to her shoulders in soft waves, bright green eyes, and a nose that turned up just slightly.

She looked as if she had tried hard not to smile, as if whoever painted the portrait had told her she must look very dignified. She wore a pale blue dress with the same kind of lacy ruffled neckline Kelly had seen on the woman in the Historic Area. Kelly stared at the portrait, thinking, That girl looks vaguely familiar. She wasn't sure why that should make her feel uneasy, but it did. She would have to ask Aunt Alma if she knew who the girl in the painting was.

Kelly jumped, startled by Jared's sudden appearance as he came around the corner from the north wing. "Have you seen the tower room yet?" Jared asked.

"Don't sneak up on me like that. This house is creepy enough."

"I think it's a neat old place." He started toward a door across from the stairs. "This probably leads up to the attic," he said. But when he turned the brass knob, the door wouldn't open.

"Why would Aunt Alma keep the attic door locked?" Kelly wondered.

Just then Aunt Alma called them down to lunch, and they forgot about the locked door and ran down the stairs. After some of the gloomier rooms upstairs and the dark front hall, the bright, cheery kitchen was a pleasant surprise. The walls were painted a lemony yellow and the cupboards were white. Double windows looked out on the magnolia trees in the backyard.

As they munched on ham and cheese sandwiches and nibbled crunchy carrot sticks, Kelly asked her aunt, "*Is* the house haunted?"

Aunt Alma looked alarmed for a moment, then said lightly, "Most old houses are haunted, wouldn't you say? And what with all the creaks and groans these old walls and floors make, shrinking and expanding, it's easy to imagine all sorts of things."

Kelly twisted a strand of hair and studied her aunt thoughtfully. Did Aunt Alma think the house was haunted or not?

"No such thing as ghosts," Jared declared between mouthfuls.

"How do you know for sure?" Kelly protested.

"It can't be scientifically proven that ghosts exist, and as far as I'm concerned, if it can't be proven using scientific methods, they don't exist."

"The trouble with you, Jared, is that you have absolutely no imagination."

"And you've got too *much.*"

"Imagination or not," Aunt Alma said, "I'm sure once this house is all fixed up, everything will be fine."

After lunch, Jared went outside to wait for Chen while Kelly ran upstairs to get her camera.

Just as she started out the door, she remembered to ask her aunt about the portrait in the upstairs hall.

Aunt Alma set her teacup down so abruptly after Kelly asked her question that the brown liquid sloshed over the rim. But Chen arrived at that moment and Jared called for Kelly to "get a move on," so she got no answer from Aunt Alma then.

Walking down the street, Kelly thought about her aunt's nervous behavior. What was Aunt Alma hiding?

Chapter 3

Kelly's troubled thoughts disappeared when she stepped onto Duke of Gloucester Street near Bruton Parish Church. The bustling scene of a re-created eighteenth-century town stretched before her.

"There's a neat graveyard on the church grounds," Chen said. "The inscriptions on the tombstones are fun to read. Some of them are nearly three hundred years old."

"I wonder if anybody who lived in Aunt Alma's house is buried there," Kelly said.

Chen shrugged. "Could be."

Next to the church was a grassy field with rows of tall trees lining either side. At the end of the green stood a large brick building surrounded by a brick wall.

"That's the Governor's Palace," Jared told Kelly. "The Palace burned down right after the American Revolution, when it was used as a hospital for American soldiers. That building was built in the 1930s when Williamsburg was restored."

Kelly glared at her brother, but Chen was obviously impressed with Jared's knowledge. "Hey, how did you know about that?" he asked.

"I'm sure he's memorized the *entire* guidebook by now," Kelly said with more than a trace of sarcasm.

Jared winked at Chen and Kelly walked off. A ways down the green, she took some shots of the impressive building.

"Come on, Kelly," Chen called. "The muster starts soon."

Kelly replaced her lens cap and started across the street, still annoyed with Jared. He was almost two years her junior and rather small for his age, but he was fond of pointing out that what he lacked in size, he made up for in brains. It seemed to Kelly that he was always trying to show off just how smart he was. She winced inwardly, thinking about the way Jared always got straight A's in school with very little effort while she, on the other hand, had barely passed this year.

It wasn't that Kelly wasn't smart, but she had little interest in studying and spent more time in her darkroom developing photographs than she did on homework. Her parents, both college professors, placed a great deal of importance on grades. It wasn't much fun to have them annoyed with her. It bothered her that they often compared her grades to Jared's and told her she wasn't working up to her potential.

Kelly supposed they were right. She sighed, recalling her father's stern words as she boarded the bus in Harrisburg, "You'll be spending the summer in one of the most historical areas of our country. Try to take advantage of the fact and absorb at least a little history while you're there."

Kelly thought history was boring, but Aunt Alma had assured her over the phone that learning about history in Colonial Williamsburg would be fun. She hoped her aunt was right.

Kelly caught up with the two boys, and they joined the crowd that was beginning to gather around the edge of the grass in front of the Magazine. Several men in eighteenth-century clothing stood near the brick wall that surrounded the Magazine. Most carried long muskets with pointed spears attached to the end. While Jared and Chen exchanged information about eighteenth-century military tactics and weapons, Kelly used the time to take pictures. Just before the program began, she spotted a familiar face in the crowd.

She nudged Jared, motioning in the direction

her camera was aimed. "There's the man who acted so weird this morning when we got off the bus."

Chen looked over at the man they were talking about. "That's Edgar Porter," he told them. "He's trying to get your aunt to sell him her house. Though why he's so anxious to buy that run-down old place is a mystery to me."

Kelly stared thoughtfully at Edgar Porter. Aunt Alma hadn't mentioned anything about selling the house. If she were thinking of selling it, she certainly wouldn't bother with a yard sale to raise money for repairs.

The men began to march and Kelly snapped more pictures. But now and then, she glanced over at the peanut-shaped man named Edgar Porter. He didn't seem to be paying much attention to the drill. He kept peering around the crowd as if he were looking for someone. Kelly wondered again why he had been so angry that morning when he thought she had taken his picture.

After the officer who had led the drill dismissed the men, Chen led Kelly and Jared to a path that went from the Historic Area to the Visitor Center, where they purchased passes that would allow them to visit the various exhibition buildings anytime during their stay in Williamsburg. When they came out of the building, the sun had disappeared behind gathering dark clouds, bringing welcome relief from the sun beating down, though the air was still heavy with humidity.

Kelly and the boys returned to the Historic Area. As they wandered down the wide main street, Chen pointed out various colonial buildings while Jared contributed bits of information he'd picked up in his reading. Kelly only half-listened to them. Her interest was in the visual charm of Colonial Williamsburg. The pretty little town was a photographer's paradise, Kelly mused. She stopped suddenly when a brown cart pulled by two fat oxen rounded the corner. The man driving the cart wore baggy blue colonial breeches and a full-sleeved, white shirt. On his head was a black, three-cornered hat like the ones so many men in the Historic Area wore.

"Hi, Richard," Chen called to the driver. Richard tipped his hat and waved. "The ox team's names are Pete and Brie. Richard is just about the only one those oxen will listen to," Chen explained. "He knows everything about oxen."

Kelly had never seen an ox before and quickly snapped several pictures. She was already on her second roll of film and could hardly wait to develop the roll she had finished. She hoped Aunt

Alma would let her set up a temporary darkroom somewhere in the house.

After a while, they headed back down the narrow side street toward Aunt Alma's house. Storm clouds filled the sky, and they walked faster when thunder rumbled in the distance.

Kelly and Jared waved goodby to Chen and climbed the rickety steps to the front porch. Inside, they were surprised to find the house so dark.

"I wonder why Aunt Alma hasn't turned on any lights," Jared said as he felt his way along the dark front hall.

"Aunt Alma," Kelly called, peering into the living room. "Boy, this is really a mess," she whispered to Jared as they threaded their way among boxes to the door on the other side of the room.

She and Jared stepped into another narrow corridor and finally found their aunt in a large parlor furnished with an odd assortment of heavy oak tables and old, faded sofas. Nothing matched, and the room looked as if over the years it had become a catchall for furniture no longer used.

"My goodness, are you back already?" Aunt Alma said in surprise. "What time is it?"

"A little after five."

"Oh, dear, and I haven't even started dinner yet. I've been trying to decide if any of these things are worth much." She waved her arms around helplessly.

"Why don't you turn on some lamps?" Jared suggested and reached toward a gaudy gold and pink ceramic lamp, minus its shade.

"I'm afraid there's no electricity in this room," Aunt Alma explained. "Only part of the house has electricity. Much of the wiring is bad, and only one circuit is working. It's a bit inconvenient, but that's one of the things I plan to remedy as soon as possible." She smiled apologetically. "I've got plenty of candles, though."

"We don't mind, do we Kelly?" Jared said quickly.

Kelly bobbed her head in agreement. "It will be kind of like an adventure." Neither Brennan cared to hurt Aunt Alma's feelings.

"Yes. Well . . . let's go into the kitchen and see about some dinner," their aunt said. "Fortunately, the kitchen is on the circuit that is working."

An hour later, they sat down to broiled chicken, mashed potatoes, and a crisp salad. Jared told his aunt about the militia muster and Kelly talked about all the wonderful pictures she'd taken.

"Aunt Alma, would it be OK if I set up a darkroom somewhere in the house?" Kelly asked. "Of course, it would have to be a room that has electricity so I can use my enlarger."

Aunt Alma assured her that would be fine and that there were several rooms that weren't being used now.

By the time they finished eating and cleaned up the kitchen, Kelly and Jared both realized how tired they were. It had been a long, busy day and they decided to go to bed before their usual bedtime.

Aunt Alma gave them each a tall candle, and they climbed the stairs to their bedrooms. The thunder was closer now. It crashed loudly following an occasional zigzag of lightning. In the upstairs hall, the flickering candlelight caught the portrait Kelly had noticed earlier that day. Kelly stopped and studied the girl's face. A flash of lightning outside the window lit the hall briefly and in that instant, Kelly felt as if she were looking into a mirror. The girl in the portrait looked exactly like her.

Chapter 4

Sometime during the night, a heavy rain began. Kelly awoke to a steady downpour beating
against her windows. There was another sound, too,
which she couldn't identify. She remembered her
aunt's words about old house creaks and groans,
and she shivered in spite of the muggy, close air of
the room. She strained her ears in an effort to pin-
point the direction from which this noise came. After listening another moment, Kelly smiled. The
sound was nothing more than the soft plop of water
dripping on the pinewood floor. Apparently the roof
leaked. She sat up and slid off the bed. Fumbling in
the dark, Kelly took a large porcelain bowl from the
dresser top to set beneath the leaking ceiling. Then
she crawled back into bed, where she lay awake for
a long time listening to the pounding rain.

The storm passed, but it continued to rain
even after Kelly and Jared finished breakfast the
next morning.

"This looks like a good day to help sort things for your yard sale, Aunt Alma," Kelly said.

"What a good idea," Aunt Alma agreed. "I'm afraid I haven't made much progress so far. There's so much old junk in this house. I don't think anybody who ever lived here threw *anything* away." She looked helplessly around the living room, then shook her head. "I don't know if it's even worth the bother. I'd have to make a great deal of money from this sale to pay all the back taxes and take care of all the renovations. My pension as a retired practical nurse doesn't allow for those sorts of expenses. Maybe I should just give up and sell it. Especially now with . . . "

"With what?" Kelly prompted.

Aunt Alma wrung her hands. "Oh, nothing. It's nothing, really."

Kelly looked at Jared, but he only shrugged and said helpfully, "How about the attic? Have you checked up there for things to sell?"

Aunt Alma's violet eyes widened in alarm. "The . . . the attic?"

"Sure. People usually store all kinds of neat stuff in attics. Would you like Kelly and me to have a look?"

Their aunt plucked a piece of lint from her purple blouse and said slowly, "I'm not sure that would be a good idea. But then, it's not as if . . . Well, I suppose it would be OK."

Jared immediately charged out of the living room and up the stairs to the second floor. Kelly followed at a slower pace. Aunt Alma sure is acting strange, she thought.

Before she reached the second floor, Jared was on his way back down the stairs. "Key," he said as he hurried past his sister.

Kelly had forgotten that the door to the attic was locked, and again she wondered why it was. Abruptly, she turned and followed Jared back into the living room, where he was asking their aunt where the attic door key was kept.

"It's on the key ring hanging by the back door in the kitchen," she told him. "But I don't remember which key fits that lock."

"Why *is* the attic locked anyway, Aunt Alma?" Kelly asked when Jared went to find the key ring.

Her aunt shrugged and mumbled, "Oh, no reason." She turned her back and lifted a small china teapot from one of the many boxes in the room. Kelly heard the teapot clatter when her aunt set it on the end table.

Upstairs, Jared tried nearly a dozen keys before one unlocked the attic door.

Kelly twisted a strand of hair around her finger, then said, "Jared, Aunt Alma is acting kind of strange, don't you think?"

Jared pushed his glasses up on his nose and shrugged. "No stranger than usual. She's always been a little bit, uh, flaky."

"But since we got here yesterday, she's been jumpy, and oh, I don't know . . . sort of on edge."

"She's just worried about the yard sale and trying to pay for all the work this place needs. And there are plenty of repairs needed, that's for sure. Do you know that the ceiling in my room leaks?"

Kelly giggled. "Mine, too."

Up in the attic, Kelly put her aunt's odd behavior out of her mind. The musty-smelling attic was one huge room cluttered with large trunks, wooden crates, stacks of newspapers and magazines, and several lopsided tables and broken chairs. It was a shadowy room. The only light came through the dust-covered dormer windows on the front roof that sloped over the room.

While Jared went back downstairs for a flashlight, Kelly tugged open the lid of a wooden trunk that was banded with decorative metal strips. The trunk, like everything else in the attic, was covered with a thick layer of dust that tickled her nose and made her sneeze.

She lifted an old, lacy dress from the trunk and held it up. Kelly thought it looked like the kind women wore in the era of the roaring twenties. Jared clumped back up the stairs carrying a large flashlight and shined it into the trunk. The entire trunk was filled with more dresses, some decorated with rows of sparkling sequins. There was also a man's tuxedo, several rather squashed top hats, and an assortment of beaded evening bags. Most of the fabrics were rotted and didn't look like they'd be worth much.

They put the clothes back and moved on to another, somewhat smaller trunk filled with dishes, mostly cracked and chipped, and a box full of letters written in spidery handwriting on thin, yellowed paper. Near the bottom of the trunk was a wooden box about the size of a shoe box. Kelly lifted it out carefully.

"Jared, look at this! It's a camera obscura."

"A what?" Jared asked, staring at the box.

"A camera obscura. The forerunner of the first camera. Look," Kelly explained, "see the mirror sticking up here? Images are reflected through the hole covered by a lens onto the frosted glass on top of the box. If you put a piece of tracing paper over the glass, you can trace the image."

Jared looked at his sister in surprise. "I've

never even *heard* of a camera obscura. How did you know that's what this was?"

Kelly smiled, pleased that for once she was the smart one. "I read a book on the history of photography last year."

"*You* actually read a book?" Jared teased. "I'm impressed."

Kelly ignored Jared's remarks and set the camera obscura aside. "Maybe later, I'll see if I can find some tracing paper and try it out."

They continued their search through the trunks and boxes and came across some pewter pitchers and several brass lamps that Kelly thought would make good sale items. While Jared carried the lamps downstairs, Kelly glanced through a box of old letters, thinking it might be fun to read some of them. She made out the date on one fragile, creased sheet of paper: September 21, 1778. So long ago! The rain was still tapping on the roof and the attic was hot and stuffy, but suddenly Kelly felt a chill in the air and she shivered.

She had the oddest feeling of being watched. I'm being silly, she told herself. She glanced around the shadowy room until her eyes fell on the camera obscura. Kelly gasped. On the frosted glass on top of the box was the image of a young girl wearing a pale blue gown with a white ruffled neckline. It was the same girl whose portrait hung in the upstairs hall.

Chapter 5

Nervously Kelly surveyed the attic, then turned back to the camera obscura. Even as she stared at the image, it grew increasingly fainter, until finally it faded completely. What was going on? When Jared came back upstairs, Kelly told him what she had seen.

Jared shook his head. "Now, let me get this straight. You looked into the—what did you call that thing, a camera obscura?" Kelly nodded. "OK. You looked into the camera obscura and you saw an image of the same person whose portrait is down in the hall." Jared looked at the old camera. "Well, there sure isn't anything there now," he pointed out.

"Of course not. I told you the image disappeared before you came back up."

"Uh . . . right. Kelly, your imagination is in high gear, as usual."

"It was *not* my imagination," Kelly insisted. "I did see the girl."

"And you also believe this house is haunted."

"It might be. I have a feeling Aunt Alma thinks so, anyway."

"It's silly to believe in ghosts," Jared stated firmly.

Kelly peered into the camera obscura, hoping the young girl would appear again so Jared could see for himself. But the glass was blank.

"I wonder who she was?" Kelly said. "I'm going to ask Aunt Alma about the portrait."

Kelly found her aunt in the downstairs tower room going through the drawers of a long buffet.

"Do you suppose anyone would buy these linen tablecloths? They're in fair condition."

Kelly told her aunt that she thought the linens should be included in the sale, then asked about the portrait.

"The portrait?" Aunt Alma said carefully.

"Yes. Do you know who she is?"

Aunt Alma nodded slowly. "It's Elizabeth Harris. The Harris family lived here in the years just before the American Revolution. She's one of our ancestors, actually." Aunt Alma looked thoughtfully at Kelly. "You resemble her, you know."

Kelly nodded. "It was kind of weird when I first realized why she looked so familiar. Do you know anything about her?"

"Not really. But I remember my grandfather mentioning something about a secret connected with the Harris family."

Kelly thought that sounded pretty exciting, but was disappointed to learn that Aunt Alma really didn't know any more about the Harris secret except that Elizabeth was involved somehow. She told her aunt about finding the camera obscura in the attic, but decided not to mention the image that had so mysteriously appeared on the glass.

They spent the rest of the morning searching through drawers and closets, and the collection of things for the yard sale grew larger and larger.

After lunch, Aunt Alma went to her room for a nap and Jared settled in the library with a biography of Thomas Jefferson. It was still drizzling outside, so Kelly decided this would be a good time to figure out where to set up a darkroom. Aunt Alma had mentioned a bathroom at the end of the south wing corridor. "Its plumbing is bad, and the fixtures didn't work well even when I visited this house as a child," she had apologized.

Now Kelly followed the long hallway to the end and opened the door to the bathroom. Perfect, she thought. The room had only one small oval window, which she could easily block out with black paper. And fortunately, this room was on the one working electrical circuit. Kelly hurried back to her bedroom to unpack the developing equipment she'd brought from home.

She worked happily for the next hour, setting up her compact enlarger and arranging various trays and chemicals. She had just replaced the lightbulb in the fixture with the red safelight she had to use when her prints were in the chemicals when there was a loud crash behind her. She let out a yelp and whirled around. The door had slammed shut. Probably pushed by a draft, she thought. But opening the door again, it occurred to her that it would take an awfully strong draft to move such a heavy door. Could Jared have sneaked down the hall and slammed the door shut to scare her? Very funny, she thought as she stomped down the hall to find him.

Kelly thought she caught a glimpse of some-one rounding the corner near the main hall, but this part of the corridor was so dim, she couldn't be sure. "Jared," she called. There was no answer.

She was about to go back to her darkroom when she heard voices downstairs in the front hall. Aunt Alma was talking to someone whose voice Kelly didn't recognize. She was halfway down the stairs before she realized that her aunt was talking to the peanut-shaped man.

"I'm sure you'll change your mind," Edgar Porter was saying. He looked up as Kelly came down the stairs.

"Mr. Porter, this is my niece, Kelly," Aunt Alma said.

Mr. Porter narrowed his eyes and stared at Kelly for a moment before saying flatly, "You're the girl with the camera."

Kelly couldn't think of a reply, and Aunt Alma looked from one to the other in confusion.

"I saw your niece over in the Historic Area yesterday," Mr. Porter said. "I . . . uh . . . I hate to have my picture taken. Uh . . . that's why I was so annoyed."

"Oh," was all Kelly could say. But she found it hard to believe anyone could dislike being photographed enough to react the way he had. Something about Edgar Porter made Kelly uneasy.

"Kelly's a wonderful photographer," Aunt Alma said quickly.

Edgar Porter raised his bushy eyebrows. "Is that so?" Then he turned back to Aunt Alma, ignoring Kelly, and said, "Let me know when you decide to sell."

Aunt Alma stiffened. "I told you I'm not at all sure I even want to sell this house. It's been in my family for generations."

Mr. Porter shrugged, saying as he started toward the front door, "I think you'll change your mind."

After she closed the door behind Edgar Porter, Aunt Alma stood there, wringing her hands.

"Is everything OK, Aunt Alma?"

"What? Oh, yes, dear. Everything's fine. No need for you to worry." She started down the hall, mumbling something about getting supper started.

Kelly stared after her aunt for a moment, then went off to find Jared.

She finally tracked him down in the downstairs tower room. When Kelly accused him of shoving the bathroom door shut, Jared insisted he hadn't even been upstairs all afternoon. Kelly still didn't believe that heavy door could have closed all by itself, but she couldn't think of any other explanation. She decided to drop the subject and tell Jared about Edgar Porter's visit.

"Why do you suppose he's so anxious to buy this wreck of a house?" she asked.

"Maybe he likes do-it-yourself projects. *Big* ones," Jared suggested.

"Maybe. But there's something strange about him. I hope Aunt Alma doesn't decide to sell this house to him."

By evening, the rain had stopped. Kelly sat on the front porch for a while, enjoying the fresh, just-washed smell that makes a summer rain so special. An occasional night bird high in a magnolia tree sang in the quiet, and quick-blinking fireflies hovered over the boxwood. It was so peaceful and pleasant on this side street that Kelly thought she could sit on the porch for hours. But when she slapped at the third mosquito in as many minutes, she decided to go indoors.

It seemed to Kelly that she hadn't been asleep long when she heard a sound outside her door. It was a kind of swishing, rustling noise. She slipped out of bed, tiptoed to her door, and opened it just enough to peek out. Moonlight streamed through the tall window at the end of the hall, making slashes of light. Down near the end of the long hall, something blue flashed around the corner. Kelly crept slowly along the corridor and peered around the corner into the main hall. Aunt Alma was standing near the attic door. She jumped when she saw her niece.

"What are you doing up at this hour?" Aunt Alma whispered.

"I thought I heard something," Kelly explained, "and when I looked out into the hall, there was something . . . " She shook her head in confusion. "I don't really know what I saw."

"I couldn't sleep," Aunt Alma told her. "I . . . I thought a glass of warm milk might help."

"Oh, then I guess it was you I saw," Kelly said. "Well, now that I'm up, I guess I'll go down to the kitchen with you. A glass of orange juice would taste good right now."

After Kelly and Aunt Alma finished their drinks in the kitchen, they climbed the stairs to their rooms. It wasn't until Kelly crawled back into bed that she had the uneasy feeling that something wasn't quite right. Suddenly, she knew what it was. Whoever she had seen at the end of the hall had been wearing something pale blue.

But Aunt Alma's bathrobe was bright red.

Chapter 6

What's going on around here? Kelly puzzled. And who or what had she seen at the end of the hall? Did the image of the girl in the camera obscura have anything to do with all these mysterious incidents?

The next morning, Kelly again pondered the odd events of the night. She dressed quickly in tan shorts and a pink T-shirt. Yesterday's rain hadn't done much to lower the temperature, and the day promised to be another scorcher. She was halfway down the stairs when she felt that something was wrong. She retraced her steps up to the wide main hall. The portrait of Elizabeth Harris was gone. Its space on the wall was bare.

That's odd, Kelly thought. She knew something about the portrait bothered Aunt Alma. Maybe her aunt had taken it down this morning. Kelly went back down the stairs and into the kitchen. The sun was shining through the kitchen window, making dappled patterns of light dance on the worn oak table. Aunt Alma was frying bacon, and just smelling it made Kelly hungry. Jared was already at the table eating his usual bowl of cereal. Kelly could never understand why he insisted on eating exactly the same thing for breakfast every single day. Two bowls of cornflakes every morning sounded pretty boring to her. As she put bread in the toaster for her aunt and herself, she asked casually, "Where did you put the portrait of Elizabeth Harris, Aunt Alma?"

Aunt Alma raised her eyebrows. "Why, you know where it is, Kelly. In the upper hall, of course."

Kelly shook her head. "Not anymore. I thought you must have taken it down for some reason."

"Oh, dear." Aunt Alma sank into a chair.

Kelly's eyes widened. "You mean you *didn't* take down the portrait?"

"N-no." Aunt Alma drummed nervously on the tabletop. "So many peculiar things happening. And now this." What was Aunt Alma talking about? Did it have something to do with the figure in blue Kelly'd seen last night? Had her aunt seen it, too? Was that one of the peculiar things she was referring to? "Aunt Alma, what's wrong?" Kelly asked.

Aunt Alma stood up suddenly. "Let's have our

breakfast. I'm sure everything will be fine. It's just my imagination, I'm sure."

Aunt Alma certainly wasn't making much sense this morning. And imagination couldn't explain a missing portrait. Kelly tried to ask her aunt what she meant about so many peculiar happenings, but Aunt Alma refused to say anything more. Instead, she suggested that Kelly and Jared explore the Historic Area this morning.

"What could have happened to the portrait?" Kelly asked her brother as they started down the sidewalk.

"I'll tell you what I think happened to it," Jared answered. "I think Aunt Alma took it down herself. She probably hung it in another room. Have you noticed how forgetful she is sometimes?"

"I don't think she moved it. Didn't you see how upset she was when I told her it wasn't hanging in the hall? Besides," Kelly added, "something really weird happened last night." She told Jared about her strange meeting with Aunt Alma in the corridor.

"And I suppose you think whatever you, and maybe Aunt Alma, saw has something to do with the missing portrait?"

"Maybe. I don't know. But there's something

odd going on and I think Aunt Alma is hiding something."

"Well, what I think is that you are letting your imagination run rampant," Jared told her firmly.

"Huh?"

"Rampant. Running wild, without restraint," Jared explained.

Kelly glared at Jared and said impatiently, "Oh, forget it. I don't want to talk to you about this if you're going to be so stubborn."

"Me stubborn? You're the one who insists on seeing ghosts who move portraits in the middle of the night. You're the one who's so sure she saw a girl's face in an old camera."

"I didn't say that what I saw last night was a ghost. But I *did* see an image in the camera obscura. And I don't care if you believe me or not. I know what I saw. So let's just drop the subject, OK?"

Jared threw up his hands. "Boy, you sure are touchy."

Kelly stomped on ahead. She knew she shouldn't let Jared get her so upset. But there *was* something strange going on. And she intended to find out just what it was. Jared caught up with her near Bruton Parish Church. She stopped so suddenly that he nearly ran into her.

Kelly turned and said calmly, "*I'm* going to visit the old graveyard Chen told us about. *You* can do whatever you want."

"I'll come along. Maybe there'll be some spirits hovering over a grave or two."

Kelly made a face at Jared and headed through the gateway in the brick wall. The grass in the churchyard was neatly trimmed, and there was a wide variety of tombstones. Some were merely small stone markers, but many were large and sat horizontally, so that they looked like stone coffins laid above the ground. Kelly strolled among the graves, stopping frequently to read the epitaphs.

Chen had been right. The inscriptions on the tombstones were interesting. "Listen to this," Kelly told Jared. "Here Lyeth Edward Dyer Who died oct. ye 6th 1722 agd 1 year & 7 Mots y Only Son of Robt Dyer & Martha his Wife."

As they wandered among the grave sites, Kelly again wondered if anyone who had once lived in Aunt Alma's house was buried here. A few minutes later, Jared pointed out the name of Josiah Harris on one of the tombstones.

"Born 1727. Died 1781. Beloved husband and father," he read.

"Harris. A relative of Elizabeth's!" Kelly said excitedly.

They spent a good bit of time reading more of the inscriptions and found other graves marked with the name Harris, but Elizabeth's was not among them.

"I want to find out more about Elizabeth and her family," Kelly said, half to herself.

"Hey," Jared said, snapping his fingers, "I just remembered something. That box of old letters we found in the attic? They must have been written by relatives or people who lived in the house."

Kelly looked at Jared in surprise. "I thought you didn't believe in ghosts?"

"I don't. But the letters are real, and Aunt Alma mentioned that the Harrises are our ancestors. It would be interesting to find out about them."

"Jared, I can't believe it, but for once I agree with you."

Jared laughed. "Let's get the letters down this evening and have a look at them."

A group was entering the old church just then, and Kelly and Jared decided to join the tour. It was cool and pleasantly refreshing inside the old church. They sat in a pew surrounded by high wooden frames and listened to the guide tell the history of Bruton Parish Church. Even Kelly found it fascinating to learn that the pews were constructed with high walls to keep out the cold winter drafts and that such men as Thomas Jefferson, Patrick Henry, and George Washington had all attended services in this church.

Before long, Kelly and Jared felt hungry and walked the three blocks back to their aunt's house. After lunch, Jared went with Chen to a nearby school yard to practice tricks on their skateboards. Kelly offered to wash the lunch dishes, after which she decided to work in her newly organized darkroom. She was anxious to see how her first pictures of Colonial Williamsburg had turned out.

On her way to the darkroom, she remembered the old letters she and Jared were going to read and decided to go up to the attic to get them now, while there was still plenty of light. She climbed the narrow staircase up to the musty attic and threaded her way among boxes and trunks until she found the one that contained the letters. As she opened the heavy lid of the trunk, she noticed the camera obscura on the floor where she'd left it. She picked it up and looked at the glass top.

Was Jared right? Had she only imagined Elizabeth's image on the glass? But even as she wondered about it, the image of Elizabeth Harris again gradually appeared on the frosted glass.

Chapter 7

After a moment, the image faded until there was nothing on the glass.

More disturbed than ever, Kelly returned to her bedroom with the letters. She took the top letter from the box. She could read the date September 13, 1777, but the ink was so faded the rest of the handwriting was almost illegible. Despite her curiosity, Kelly replaced the letter in the box, deciding to wait until later, when she and Jared could both try to decipher the old script. Maybe Aunt Alma would want to help, too.

Kelly spent the next few hours in her darkroom doing what she enjoyed most—transforming a roll of black negatives into wonderful real-life pictures. She used tongs to lift each print out of the developing tray and into the stop bath, then into the rinsing tray. The pictures she had snapped of Richard driving the oxcart were great. She had caught the oxen just as they lumbered toward her, their hulking bodies gently swaying as they plodded down the street.

When she lifted the picture she'd taken, more or less accidently, of Edgar Porter out of the rinsing bath, she noticed something rather odd. When she'd focused her camera on Mr. Porter, she'd thought he was studying a guide map. But in the photograph, the paper he was holding didn't look like any of the Colonial Williamsburg guide maps Jared was always examining. After hanging up the print to dry, she slipped the negative back into the carrier of the enlarger.

This time she concentrated on the portion of the negative that showed the large paper Mr. Porter held. She turned the head control to blow up that particular section, set the timer, and pushed the switch for the exposure. When the enlarger switched off, she transferred the developing paper to the chemical tray and waited for the picture to emerge. When the image was sharp, she used tongs to lift the paper from the chemical solution into the stop bath to end the developing process, then into the rinse water to wash off any chemical residue.

While the print was in the wash, Kelly switched on the overhead light, then hung the print to dry. Now, studying the enlargement, she saw that her suspicion had been right. Edgar Porter was definitely not holding a Colonial Williamsburg guide map. The paper appeared to be some sort of blueprint. But a blueprint of what? It could be house plans, Kelly mused. A friend of her father's had once shown them the plans for a house he wanted to build, and those plans looked very much like the paper the peanut-shaped man was holding. But why was Mr. Porter studying house plans in the middle of the Historic Area? Even if he was planning to build a house, would he carry the blueprints around with him when he was sightseeing?

Kelly cleaned up her work area and washed the trays and tongs, still puzzling over the photograph of Edgar Porter looking at a blueprint. Then she went to find Aunt Alma and see if she needed any help. The house was so large that it was hard telling in which room Aunt Alma might now be collecting things to add to the yard sale.

Kelly checked the bedroom and study across the hall from her room, then followed the dim corridor to the main upper hall. Aunt Alma had mentioned wanting to look in the small sitting room adjoining the upstairs tower room. Kelly turned the corner and followed yet another shadowy corridor. There was no electricity in this part of the upstairs, and the windowless hall was almost as dark as night. Kelly shivered and walked faster, calling out her aunt's name.

The sitting room was empty, so she went on into the tower room. It was a smallish, round room with a wrought-iron staircase leading to the tower room below. Two tall, narrow windows, though covered with dust, let in a fair amount of sunlight. The only furnishings in the room were a love seat, a pair of shabby high-backed chairs, and a tall chest of drawers. On one wall was a faded tapestry stitched in threads of red, gold, and green that depicted what looked like a court scene of some sort. On the opposite wall was a large portrait that made Kelly suck in her breath.

It was the missing portrait of Elizabeth Harris. How had it gotten in here? Could Aunt Alma have moved it and then forgotten about it, as Jared had suggested?

Kelly backed out of the room and sped along the dim hallway and down the stairs. She found Aunt Alma on the front porch, sipping iced tea from a tall glass.

"Hello, dear. How did your photographs turn out?" Aunt Alma asked.

"Huh?" Kelly had forgotten for the moment about her pictures and the darkroom. "Oh, great. I'll show you later, after they've dried." She took a deep breath. "Aunt Alma, the portrait's back. I found Elizabeth Harris hanging in the tower room."

Aunt Alma's face turned chalky white, and with a shaking hand she set her glass down on the little table beside her wicker chair. "Oh, dear."

"Aunt Alma," Kelly asked gently, "are you *sure* you didn't move the portrait yourself? I mean, you've had a lot on your mind lately—the yard sale and all. Maybe—"

"My dear girl, I know properly well that I occasionally forget things. But," Aunt Alma insisted firmly, "I did *not* move that portrait from the hall into the tower room."

Kelly nodded. "I didn't really think you did. Did you notice if the portrait was still hanging in the hall when you got up in the middle of the night last night?"

Aunt Alma shook her head. "No, I didn't notice. I . . . I guess I wasn't paying much attention to portraits at the time."

"I didn't notice, either," Kelly admitted. "Do you want me to hang the portrait back in the hall?"

Aunt Alma looked startled, then said, "Yes. Let's go do that right now."

As they carried the portrait from the tower room to its proper place in the upper hall, Kelly asked her aunt if she'd seen anything unusual last night. Aunt Alma adjusted the portrait and didn't answer.

"Something or somebody in blue?" Kelly persisted.

Aunt Alma sighed and sank down on a straight-backed walnut side chair. "I didn't want to worry you and Jared about all this, but it sounds like you've seen it, too, so I might as well tell you." She paused as if gathering her thoughts. "For the past couple of weeks, some rather peculiar things have been happening around here, things that I can't find any logical explanation for."

"Like what?"

"Well, for one thing, there's the scent of lilacs in my bedroom. It's not there all the time, but often when I walk into the room, it's as if someone wearing lilac-scented perfume had been there. And then there are the noises. I sometimes wake up during the night and hear a swishing sound. It makes me think of someone going down the hall wearing a long, full gown and brushing against the wall. It's a soft rustling sound."

"I . . . I heard that sound last night too," Kelly stammered.

Aunt Alma nodded. "And yes, I've seen the figure in blue, too. And now the portrait disappears

58

from the hall and turns up in the tower room. It's all rather frightening."

Kelly's gaze shifted from her aunt to the portrait on the wall. "Aunt Alma," she said slowly, "look at the portrait. Elizabeth's gown is pale blue."

Chapter 8

Y es," Aunt Alma said. "I've wondered if there's some connection between the portrait of Elizabeth and the figure in blue."

"Have you seen her face—I mean the face of the person we both saw last night?"

"Not really, except a glimpse of it the night I saw her open the attic door. I locked the door after that."

Kelly wanted to tell her aunt about seeing Elizabeth's image in the camera obscura. She knew Aunt Alma wouldn't laugh the way Jared had, but the frightened look on her aunt's face stopped her.

"I just don't know what to do. I've loved this house since I was a little girl, and I was so pleased when Uncle Edward left it to me. Now I'm afraid that between all the repairs that are needed and all these peculiar goings on . . . it's more than I can cope with." She shook her head. "I'm beginning to think selling the house might be wise after all."

"What about a bank loan?"

"I've already looked into loans and mortgages. But the banks don't consider someone with only a small pension a good risk. And loan payments on top of all those back taxes to pay." Aunt Alma sighed and stood up. "It'd be just too much to manage."

Kelly tried to think of something to say. "I'm sure everything will be all right." Kelly wasn't sure what she meant by that, but it was the best she could do.

"Of course, dear. I'm just being a silly old woman." Aunt Alma straightened her shoulders. "Let's go get dinner started."

Down in the kitchen, Kelly sliced tomatoes for a salad and Aunt Alma bustled about putting together ingredients for spaghetti sauce. While they worked, Kelly told her about the old letters she and Jared had found in the attic. "We're going to read them tonight. Maybe we can find out something about the people who lived in this house. Do you want to help?"

Aunt Alma agreed that it would be fun reading old letters. After dinner, Kelly got the box from her room and carried it out onto the large, screened-in porch. There was a pleasant breeze ruffling the broad leaves of the magnolia trees, and the evening air was a bit cooler than the heat of the day.

Reading the old-fashioned handwriting proved to be slow going. Often words or even entire sentences were illegible, and the unfamiliar spellings of many words added to the challenge. Some of the letters were from relatives in England who were shocked at the news from the colonies. One person wrote that *this disagreement with our good King George is a disgrace.*

"Listen to this letter," Jared said. *"Everything is going according to plan. I agree. The situation in the colonies has become intolerable. Help will soon be forthcoming.* The letter is written to Josiah Harris from William somebody. The last name is blurred."

"What kind of help do you suppose he meant?" Kelly asked.

"Wait a minute," Jared said excitedly, "there's more. *The ship should arrive by the end of summer. We hope to reach Virginia before bad weather is upon us. Tell Benjamin we may need his help. The—* the word is smudged—*should be sufficient to purchase a good many arms. King George must learn that he cannot successfully rule our country from afar."* Jared set the letter down. "Wow. Sounds like some sort of secret plan to help the colonies oppose the king's soldiers. Maybe that's what Aunt

Alma's grandfather meant by a secret in the family."

"But," Kelly wondered, "what was being sent by ship?"

"Some kind of money, obviously. The letter talks about purchasing arms. Maybe it was gold."

Aunt Alma set down the letter she had been trying to read. "This elaborate script is a bit much for my old eyes."

Kelly and Jared skimmed through several more letters, but learned nothing further about the plan to help the patriots. They did learn that Elizabeth's father had owned some sort of small shop in Williamsburg, and one letter was from a cousin inviting Elizabeth to visit her at a near-by plantation. It wasn't until they reached the bottom of the box that they found the diary.

Kelly opened the small book to the first page and read, "Elizabeth Ann Harris, 1776." She looked up, her green eyes bright with excitement. "This is actually Elizabeth's own diary!" Without waiting for a reply from Jared or her aunt, Kelly began reading. Elizabeth's handwriting wasn't quite as spidery as that in some of the letters, but it still took real effort to make out all the words. Elizabeth wrote that Williamsburg was full of excitement that summer and everyone was talking about the document that Mr. Jefferson had written.

"That must be the Declaration of Independence," Jared said. "What's the date of that entry?"

"August 23, 1776," Kelly answered. "And listen to this: *A great many people are glad that we have declared ourselves free and independent from England. But others, like Mr. John Randolph, are calling it treason against His Majesty, King George. Papa says there are still others who aren't certain who's right or wrong in the matter, but he believes the colonies should no longer tolerate the foolish abuses from our mother country. He told me that as a patriot, he will do what he can to help achieve true independence.*" Kelly looked up from the diary, frowning. "That's strange. I thought everybody wanted independence."

Jared chuckled and told her smugly, "You should have paid attention in history class. Not everybody felt independence was a good thing. Lots of people felt a great loyalty to the king of England. After all, the Virginians were English."

Kelly thought about that for a moment, then shrugged.

It was growing too dark on the porch to see, so Kelly closed the diary and put it aside. Aunt Alma brought out a tray of cold lemonade and chocolate chip cookies. As Kelly nibbled on a cookie, she absently swatted a mosquito and thought about the letters and Elizabeth's diary. What was it like living during the 1700s? she wondered. "I wonder why Elizabeth isn't buried in the Bruton Parish Church graveyard?" she murmured, half to herself.

"Maybe she married and moved away from Williamsburg," Aunt Alma suggested.

"Right. Or, even if she married and stayed here in town, her name wouldn't have been Harris," Jared pointed out.

"Oh." Kelly was annoyed not to have thought of that herself.

"Unless, of course, she married a cousin with the same last name," Jared continued.

When Kelly raised her eyebrows, Aunt Alma said, "Yes, it was quite common for cousins to marry in those days."

"How old do you suppose Elizabeth was when that portrait was painted?"

"It's hard to say," her aunt replied, "but I'd guess probably not more than fourteen or fifteen."

As they finished the last of the cookies, the first stars appeared in the dark summer sky. Kelly gazed up through the trees and wondered if Elizabeth would appear that night. In the last few hours, she had really begun to believe that the fleeting figure in blue was Elizabeth Harris's ghost. After reading from Elizabeth's diary, she felt that she was beginning to know her a little. And, although she knew the idea of having a ghost in the house made Aunt Alma uneasy, Kelly felt sure Elizabeth's ghost meant no harm.

At least she hoped not.

Chapter 9

Bright slashes of sunlight streamed through the high curved windows. Kelly dressed quickly in gray shorts and a blue T-shirt with the word "Shutterbug" printed on the front, then hurried downstairs to the kitchen. She wanted to ask Aunt Alma if she'd heard or seen anything during the night, but decided not to upset her further.

"Is it all right if I go over to the Historic Area this morning, Aunt Alma?" Kelly asked as she spread thick strawberry jam on an English muffin. "I'd like to take some more photographs."

"That's fine, dear. I'm going to visit a friend."

Kelly finished her breakfast, helped Aunt Alma wash the dishes, then ran upstairs to get her camera and extra film. She planned to take a series of photographs showing the various tradespeople at work in their shops. As she walked the few blocks to the Historic Area, she decided to start with the apothecary, which, Jared had told her, was an eighteenth-century pharmacy.

The buildings had just opened for the day, but already Duke of Gloucester Street was crowded with visitors. Kelly stopped to watch a green and gold carriage head down the street and wondered if Elizabeth Harris and her family had owned a carriage like that. And again Kelly fell to musing over the strange appearances of Elizabeth. Why was her ghost haunting Aunt Alma's house? Ghosts usually appeared for some specific reason, didn't they?

As she climbed the steps to the apothecary, Kelly pushed thoughts of Elizabeth from her mind and entered the world of eighteenth-century medicine. The young woman behind the counter talked about many of the medical practices of two hundred years ago. Kelly took several pictures of the woman showing the visitors old-fashioned wooden splints and bleeding instruments. Kelly shuddered when she looked into a jar of live leeches like those used to remove what people long ago thought of as bad blood. She left the shop, thankful that doctors today knew much more about medicines and treatments than they did back in the 1700s.

From the apothecary, she walked across the street to the wigmaker's shop. There she learned that before you could be fitted for a wig, you first had to have your head completely shaved in order to ensure a tight fit for your wig. No thanks, Kelly thought. She used her zoom lens to get a close-up of the wigmaker weaving thin strands of dark brown hair into a wig.

Next she strolled across the street to visit the printer and bookbinder. In the garden behind the two shops, she watched a man dressed in baggy brown breeches and white shirt make paper from cotton rags. Kelly asked him several questions while she snapped pictures of each step involved in the old-time process of paper making. She listened to the man's explanations carefully, thinking how proud her father would be when she showed him the photographs and was able to explain what was happening in each one. Kelly smiled. In spite of herself, she was learning quite a bit of history this summer.

As she climbed the steep stairs back up to Duke of Gloucester Street, Kelly had to squint at the sudden harsh glare of the sun after the cool shade down in the garden beside the Printing Office. She found a wooden bench beneath a tall sugar maple and sat down. For several minutes, she watched the crowds of people wandering up and down Duke of Gloucester Street.

Just as she stood to join the people entering the silversmith's shop, she spied a face in the crowd. His dark hair was as wild and bushy as ever. He narrowed his eyes when he saw Kelly and crossed the street. "Well, if it isn't the junior photographer," he said.

"Hello, Mr. Porter," Kelly said casually. "Doing some more sightseeing?"

He looked surprised at the question. "Huh?"

Kelly waved her arms around to indicate the exhibition buildings.

"Oh, right. Actually, I have some business to take care of," Edgar Porter said vaguely.

Kelly wondered what kind of business he had to take care of in the Historic Area, but she didn't ask or comment.

"Has your aunt decided to sell her house yet?" Mr. Porter's eyes darted here and there as he talked to Kelly.

"Why do you want to buy Aunt Alma's house anyway? I mean, it's really in terrible shape."

Edgar Porter glared at Kelly. "That's really none of your business, is it, little girl? But if you must know, I happen to be interested in old houses. Your aunt's house has a certain charm to it." With that, he turned and walked away.

Kelly shrugged. Somehow Mr. Porter's use of the word "charm" didn't fit him. And, although she couldn't exactly say why, she didn't believe him.

More than ever, Kelly distrusted this man.

She decided to head back to the house. With the sun directly overhead, the heat was stifling. Besides, she was starving. The thought of a thick sandwich of Virginia ham and sliced fresh tomatoes along with a glass of cold lemonade was very appealing.

Jared was already in the kitchen eating a peanut butter sandwich when Kelly walked in. She told him about talking to Edgar Porter. "There's something very strange about that man," she said.

"I can't imagine why he wants this old house, either. And I hope Aunt Alma will make enough money on her yard sale so she won't have to sell to him."

"Do you really think the yard sale could bring in *that* much money?" Kelly asked.

Jared shrugged and pushed his glasses up on his nose with his thumb. "Probably not. You know what Mom's yard sales are like. People come looking for bargains. She usually ends up selling things really cheap just to get rid of them."

"Right. And that's probably what will happen at Aunt Alma's sale, too." Kelly took a bite of her sandwich and chewed thoughtfully for a moment. "I wish we could think of some way to help her keep the house. She gets really sad whenever the subject of selling it comes up."

After lunch, Kelly went up to her room and curled up on the plump green-cushioned window seat with Elizabeth's diary. Kelly learned that the tension in Williamsburg increased as the year 1776 came to an end. Elizabeth's entry of January 14, 1777, said, *Papa hopes his plan to help the patriot soldiers will work.* Kelly continued reading, but there was no further mention of the plan. She wondered what sort of plan it was and whether it had worked or not.

She skimmed the next several pages, then something caught her eye. *The British soldiers came to the door again, looking for Papa and demanding to know what we have done with the gold. I'm so frightened. Papa told me before he and Benjamin left that I was not to tell anyone where the coins are hidden. I told the soldiers that Papa and Benjamin are away on business, but they didn't believe me. And now, Mama has taken ill and I don't know what to do. What if they force their way into the house and search for the gold? The coins are well hidden in the very depths of darkness. At least I hope so.*

Gold! Gold coins hidden somewhere in this very house! Kelly ran into the hall, the old diary still clutched in her hand. "Jared," she shouted, "where are you?" Kelly continued shouting as she flew down the stairs. Almost at the same time, Jared popped his head out of the library and Aunt Alma rushed into the hall from the kitchen.

"What are you bellowing about? Have you just seen another ghost?" Jared demanded.

Kelly ignored her brother's sarcasm. "Just wait until you hear this," she cried. "You are not going to believe it!"

Chapter 10

Gold! Hidden in this house," Kelly exclaimed breathlessly after she read the excerpt from Elizabeth's diary to Jared and her aunt.

Jared stared calmly at his sister. "Kelly, you're talking about something that happened more than two hundred years ago."

"But suppose the coins were never found? Suppose they're still here somewhere?" Kelly's green eyes sparkled and the pitch of her voice rose with each sentence. "Aunt Alma, have you ever heard anything about gold coins hidden in this house?"

Aunt Alma ran a plump hand through her gray hair. "Why, yes," she said slowly. "I'd forgotten all about that story, though. Great-grandfather Maxwell used to entertain my brother and me with all sorts of tales when we visited here. Of course, he was quite elderly at the time, and my mother cautioned us not to take his stories too seriously."

"Aunt Alma," Kelly practically shrieked, "what *was* the story about the gold coins?"

"Oh. Now, let me think. I remember Great-grandfather saying how brave our ancestors were. And something about someone smuggling gold coins from England. I think the gold was meant to be used to outfit American soldiers." She paused, then said apologetically, "I'm afraid that's all I remember."

"But what happened to the gold?" Kelly wanted to know.

Aunt Alma shook her head. "I don't remember Great-grandfather ever saying. I suppose no one ever knew what became of the coins."

"Then they *could* still be here in the house!" Kelly said eagerly.

"Not likely," Jared said. "A lot of different people have lived here since then. If the gold was left here, chances are it would have been found before now."

"I'm afraid Jared's right," Aunt Alma agreed. "Somebody would have discovered those coins long ago."

"But, Aunt Alma, just think. If the coins are still here and if we can find them, you'd have plenty of money to fix up the house. Old gold coins would be worth a fortune today. You wouldn't have to sell to Mr. Porter."

"My dear, that's a lovely thought. But I'm afraid it's only wishful thinking."

"Kelly, I hate to keep repeating myself, but once again, your—"

"Don't you dare say it, Jared Brennan," Kelly cut in. "Don't you *dare* tell me my imagination is running wild again."

Jared whooped and slapped his thigh. "Looks like I don't have to say it. You just did."

"Oooh," Kelly sputtered, "you . . . you . . . "

"Now, now," Aunt Alma said, "there's no sense quarreling over something that happened so long ago. Kelly, you know Jared is only teasing. And Jared," she added, "there's nothing wrong with having a healthy imagination."

There was a knock on the door just then. Chen appeared and asked Jared if he wanted to go over to the school yard with his skateboard. After Jared left, Kelly wandered into the kitchen to find a snack. While she spread peanut butter and banana slices on bread, she thought, The gold coins *could* still be hidden in this house somewhere. She picked up Elizabeth's diary and continued reading from where she'd left off.

The next couple of entries made no mention of the gold or Elizabeth's father's plan. Elizabeth did, however, write that she was worried because her father and Benjamin had not yet returned.

Kelly turned the page, impatient to learn more. *Two very stern British soldiers pounded on the door today,* Kelly read. *They were quite rude and insisted upon speaking to Papa. I don't think they believed me when I said he was still away on business. They demanded to know what we have done with the gold. One of the men spoke in a particularly harsh manner and said he would return tomorrow with more soldiers. He assured me they intend to make a thorough search of the house. I'm so frightened. Papa said I must tell no one where the gold is.*

Kelly turned the next page eagerly. But to her surprise, it was blank. She flipped quickly through the remaining pages of the diary and discovered they were *all* blank. That had been Elizabeth's last entry. It was dated July 2, 1781.

Why hadn't Elizabeth written in the diary again? Had the British soldiers come back to the house? Had they found the coins? Kelly's head spun with questions. But the one uppermost in her mind was whether gold coins hidden more than two hundred years ago could still be somewhere in this house.

Chapter 11

The next morning, Kelly and Jared helped Aunt Alma price the furniture for the sale. While they fastened tags on broken chairs and wobbly tables, Kelly told them about Elizabeth's last diary entry and how the rest of the diary was nothing but blank pages.

"I really think it's possible those old coins are still here somewhere," Kelly said.

"Forget it," Jared said. "That's crazy."

"I agree it's an exciting idea, dear. But Jared is probably right. The gold would hardly still be in this house after so many years." Aunt Alma lifted some dishes from a box and mumbled, "Though, goodness knows, a few pieces of gold lying around here would be more than welcome."

Kelly wrinkled her forehead and tugged on a lock of hair. "I wish we knew more about Elizabeth and her family."

"The library," Jared said thoughtfully. "Chen

says Colonial Williamsburg has a special research library. Old family records, account books, that kind of stuff. Maybe there's some sort of record about the Harris family."

"Why, what a good idea," Aunt Alma said. "The library isn't too far from the Historic Area. Chen could show you where it is."

Kelly looked at her brother in admiration. "Jared, that's a terrific idea."

Jared bowed. "Naturally."

That afternoon, Kelly, Jared, and Chen stood at the door of the large, modern building that housed the Colonial Williamsburg Foundation Library.

"Just let me do the talking," Jared said as they entered the building. Kelly looked at her younger brother, annoyed that he insisted on being in charge. "Take it easy," Jared said, catching her look. "You know when you get excited, you don't make a lot of sense."

Kelly was too angry to answer. One of these days she would prove to Jared that she was just as smart as he was.

They followed signs that led to the library. The room didn't look like the public library back home. Men and women sat at desks in cubicles where they answered phones or tapped computer keyboards. There were large flat file drawers holding old maps and prints and a large wall unit with a revolving display that held slides of scenes taken in the Historic Area.

Beyond one wall was a separate glassed-in room that housed rare books that had survived from the eighteenth century. The room was humidity-controlled to preserve the fragile old paper and bindings. Several other small rooms adjoined the large main room and contained an assortment of odd-looking machines. At the far end of the room there were numerous shelves holding hundreds of books about the eighteenth century and Virginia history.

Jared marched across the carpeted floor to the woman seated behind the information desk and explained what they wanted to know.

The librarian thought for a moment, then said, "Well, Williamsburg was occupied by the British at the end of the Revolutionary War, from June 27 until July 4, 1781. But if you want to know about a particular family, I think you should start with our microfilm files. Our staff has researched a number of old Williamsburg families and much of the information has been put on microfilm. I don't know how much we have on the specific Harrises you're interested in, but I do know that there were a number of Harrises in Williamsburg during the eighteenth century."

She led them to an area that was lined with gray metal file drawers. She pulled out a drawer, explaining that the cards were arranged alphabetically by subject and names.

"Here we are," she said, "Harris." After locating the correct microfilm reel, she led them over to a microfilm viewer. The librarian loaded the film and demonstrated how the controls worked to move the film backward and forward.

Jared promptly claimed the chair directly in front of the machine and began moving the scanner. Kelly and Chen peered over his shoulder, trying to read the words on the screen. The first page listed an Edmond Harris, born 1688, Sussex, England. His wife was listed, although her date of birth was unknown, and the names of six children. Four had died in infancy, but two sons, John, born 1721, and Josiah, born 1727, had left England and settled in Virginia. As they continued turning the control knob forward, they learned that Josiah Harris had married Anne Sawyer and had two children, Benjamin, born 1760, died date unknown, and Elizabeth, born 1766, died 1781.

Jared turned the knob, moving the microfilm forward, but Kelly grabbed his arm. "Elizabeth! That's *our* Elizabeth!"

Jared nodded. "And she mentioned a brother Benjamin in the diary, too. So it looks like we've found the right Harris family."

"Quick," Kelly said, "turn the screen back, Jared." Jared moved the knob back until Kelly said, "Stop there! Oh, my gosh. Look at that date."

Jared and Chen stared at the screen. Jared shrugged. "What about it?"

"Elizabeth died July 3, 1781."

"So?"

"*So,* her last diary entry was *July 2, 1781.* She died the very day after that last entry was written."

Chen looked at the screen. "Wow, I wonder what happened? Do you suppose she was sick or something?"

"That's possible," Jared said thoughtfully. "In her diary, she mentioned that her mother was ill. She could have come down with the same illness. People in those days died from things we consider relatively minor."

But Kelly shook her head. "Even if she'd gotten sick, it doesn't seem likely she would have died less than a day later. Besides, she never mentioned not feeling well. What she did say in that last entry was that she was frightened because the British soldiers had threatened to come back and search the house the next day."

"Hmmn . . . " Jared took his glasses off and absently polished them on his T-shirt. "I wonder what really happened the next day. I wonder how she died."

"Suppose the British soldiers did go back to the house. Maybe they forced their way inside. Maybe one of them shoved Elizabeth out of the way and she fell and hit her head, and maybe they never found the gold because they had to leave Williamsburg the next day. And maybe she didn't get buried in the Bruton Parish graveyard because her mom was sick and her dad and brother weren't there and there was all this confusion from the British leaving. Maybe—"

"And maybe you're getting carried away again," Jared interrupted. But his face was slightly flushed and he cracked his knuckles, the way he did when he was excited or intrigued about something.

They scanned the rest of the microfilm roll, but found out only that Benjamin married a woman named Sally Harrison and that they had five children. There was no further mention of Elizabeth.

"Well," Kelly said after they left the library, "we still don't know anything more about the gold coins."

They headed toward the Historic Area, and Kelly told the boys what Aunt Alma had told her about seeing a figure wearing a pale blue gown just like the one Elizabeth was wearing in the portrait.

"Hey," Chen said, "it sounds like that old house really *is* haunted."

"Nonsense," Jared said. "Aunt Alma is just imagining things. Maybe," he added to Kelly with a twinkle in his eye, "wild imaginations run in the family."

"Look, Mr. Know-It-All, for your information, I also saw a figure in blue and heard the same rustling sounds Aunt Alma heard. It's not likely two different people would imagine exactly the *same* thing, is it?"

Jared shrugged. "Power of suggestion." But Kelly thought he sounded less confident than usual.

Chapter 12

"I f you want to find out about ghosts, you should visit the Peyton Randolph House," Chen said when they reached the Historic Area. "It's supposed to be full of ghosts and spirits."

Kelly glanced quickly at Chen, not sure if he, too, was teasing her. But Chen smiled and told her that an old friend of his mother's swore she'd seen a man dressed in colonial garb standing at the top of the main stairs in the house.

"And some of the guides who have worked there for a long time say they've seen a woman in the oak-paneled bedroom upstairs."

"Oh, brother," Jared groaned. "Don't tell me you're going along with my sister and her wacky ghost theory?"

Chen ran his hand through his thick black hair. "I didn't exactly say I believe in ghosts. But I don't exactly *not* believe, either. Guess you could say I like to keep an open mind."

Jared shook his head. "OK, let's go see these ghosts." And when they reached the old home, Jared marched up to the front door of the Peyton Randolph House. He showed his pass to a pretty young woman wearing a rose-colored colonial gown.

Inside, they looked around the parlor and the adjoining workroom from which Mrs. Randolph had run her household, then climbed the winding back stairs to the second floor. Chen led the way through several small rooms to the doorway of the infamous oak bedchamber. Kelly stared into the room for several minutes, but was disappointed not to see even a wispy figure. There was another guide in the upstairs hall, and Kelly approached her.

"Excuse me, I was wondering about . . . uh, ghosts. I mean . . . my friend said this house is supposed to have a couple of ghosts roaming around." Kelly stopped, feeling a little silly.

The guide nodded. "According to the old stories, this house is inhabited by several different spirits."

Kelly's eyes widened and she asked eagerly, "Have you ever seen any of them?"

"No," the woman said, "but I've talked to people who claim that the oak bedchamber is home to an old woman who stands at the foot of the bed, wringing her hands and trying to speak."

"Who is she?"

"Nobody seems to know. Apparently, a number of tragedies occurred in this house over the years. Many people believe the ghosts here are connected somehow to those events. Not many of our visitors know about the ghost stories connected with this house, but oddly enough, you're the second person in just a few minutes to ask about ghosts."

Kelly thanked the woman and joined Chen and Jared across the hall. This room was the principal bedchamber. Two high-post beds with hand-stitched counterpanes and curtains took up most of the space. An open-hearth fireplace was centered on the opposite wall. Kelly gazed at the dressing table positioned between two windows on the side wall and wondered if Elizabeth had sat at a similar dressing table and fashioned her hair with tortoiseshell brushes and combs like those on the table.

A pair of bulky hoops, worn under eighteenth-century gowns to make them stand out, were draped over a stool. Kelly was glad that girls today wore more comfortable clothing. She turned from the room and headed down the main staircase.

Near the bottom of the stairs she saw a familiar figure standing by the back door. Quickly, Kelly raised her camera and pretended to focus on the colorful flower arrangement on the hall table. At the same moment, Edgar Porter turned and caught sight of Kelly on the stairs. Without a word, he whirled around and ducked out the back door. Kelly crossed the hall into the large, elegantly furnished dining room and, after taking a few pictures, joined the boys, who were already outside. She told them what the guide had said about ghosts and about seeing Mr. Porter in the hall.

"We saw him, too. In fact, Mr. Porter bolted out the door as if *he* had just seen a ghost." Jared chuckled. "You have a strange effect on him, Kelly."

Kelly made a face at Jared, then said, "I wonder where he lives."

"Your aunt told my mom he's only been in town a couple of months and that he's renting a furnished apartment out on Jamestown Road," Chen said.

"What does he do for a living?"

"I think he's retired from the navy, but I'm not sure what he does now."

Jared wanted to visit the Raleigh Tavern, so they crossed Market Square back onto Duke of Gloucester Street. Despite the uncomfortable heat and humidity, the street was crowded with tourists and the lines of people waiting outside the exhibition buildings were long. As they joined the group waiting to enter the old tavern, Kelly brushed a strand of damp hair off her forehead. To take her mind off the heat while they were waiting, she decided to take some more photographs. She snapped several shots of the crowds moving slowly along the street and a few of the outside of the tavern.

Finally, the front door of the Raleigh Tavern opened and a costumed guide invited the group in. The rush of cool air as they entered the building was more than a little welcome. Along with the other visitors Kelly listened to the woman describe the importance of taverns in the community two hundred years ago.

Kelly was surprised to learn that the tavern had provided not only food and drink for people in Williamsburg, but overnight lodging for travelers as well. The tavern also served as a meeting place where folks could learn the latest news from other areas and discuss political matters and local gossip. Occasionally, balls and other social events had taken place in the Raleigh Tavern.

A few minutes later, the guide led them upstairs to see the part of the tavern that had served as a hotel. As she climbed the stairs, Kelly wondered if Elizabeth's father had once sat in the tavern and discussed the secret plan to help the patriots in their fight against England.

When they reached the famous Apollo Room, Kelly tried to imagine what this room had looked like in 1776. She could almost see it filled with men wearing ruffled shirts and elaborate waistcoats and breeches. Some men probably voiced their opinions in loud, booming voices as they tried to persuade people loyal to England to their way of thinking. Others, maybe Elizabeth's father, might have whispered secret plans to friends.

Jared nudged Kelly when it was time to move on into the billiard room. Kelly came out of her eighteenth-century daydream with a sigh. What really had happened to the hidden gold? she again wondered.

It was nearly five o'clock when they left the tavern, so they went back to Aunt Alma's house. Their aunt was sitting on the front porch, and Kelly immediately told her what they'd found out at the library.

"Don't you think it's odd that Elizabeth died so suddenly?" Kelly asked her aunt.

"It does seem rather strange. But I don't suppose we'll ever know what really happened, will we? But," she added, "let's not worry about all that tonight. We've been working hard getting ready for the yard sale, and I've decided we deserve a treat. I've made reservations at Chowning's Tavern for dinner. I want you to taste some authentic Colonial Williamsburg cooking."

Dinner at a colonial tavern sounded terrific to Kelly, but she couldn't forget Elizabeth and the exciting possibility of hidden gold somewhere in this old house. More disturbing was the nagging puzzle of what had happened to Elizabeth after she wrote in her diary on July 2.

Chapter 13

C howning's Tavern was crowded. Luckily Aunt
Alma had phoned early for reservations. A
young man wearing dark gray breeches and a green
waistcoat over the familiar white, baggy-sleeved
shirt led them to their table. Blue and gray stone-
ware mugs sat on the wooden tables, and candlelight cast a soft glow in the room.

Kelly studied the menu trying to decide what
to order, but Jared barely looked at his menu. "I'd
like a hamburger, please," he said.

"Surely, you're not serious? You must try some
of the tavern's colonial dishes," Aunt Alma said.

"No, thanks. A hamburger will be fine."

"But, Jared—"

"Forget it, Aunt Alma," Kelly said, laughing.
"You'll never convince Jared to try anything new or
unusual in the way of food. When it comes to eating, he's not at all curious."

"At least I'm not into bizarre concoctions like

those peanut butter and banana sandwiches you claim are so delicious," Jared scoffed.

Aunt Alma listened to this exchange, then asked Jared, "So, you really want a *hamburger?*" Jared nodded.

"Don't worry, Aunt Alma," Kelly said. "*I'd* like to try some colonial food."

Aunt Alma patted Kelly's arm. "Why don't we start with cheese and sippets. Virginians have been eating sippets since the seventeenth century."

After they'd ordered, the waiter brought a crock of Cheddar cheese accompanied by "sippets," toasted strips of bread. Even Jared pronounced the sippets "pretty good."

After the cheese and sippets, Jared's hamburger arrived, along with the Brunswick stew Kelly and Aunt Alma had ordered. "This is delicious," Kelly said.

Jared grinned mischievously at his sister. "Bet you don't even know what's in that, do you?" Kelly shrugged and went on eating. "Squirrel!" Jared said. "You are eating squirrel."

Kelly put her fork down. "Squirrel? There's squirrel in this stew?"

Jared's triumphant whoop caused diners around them to stare. Apparently the waiter had heard them, because he paused by their table.

"The original Brunswick stew recipe had squirrel in it," he explained, "but we use chicken." With a grin, he continued on his way.

Kelly glared at her brother. "You're such a child, Jared Brennan. Why don't you just be quiet and eat your *boring* hamburger." Then, determinedly, she ate more of the stew.

When they had finished the main course, Kelly and Aunt Alma ordered pecan tarts for dessert and Jared chose vanilla ice cream.

"That was wonderful, Aunt Alma," Kelly said after they had finished eating. "Thanks for bringing us here."

While Aunt Alma sipped her tea, Kelly looked around the room. She wished she had brought her camera. The room lit with shadowy candlelight would make an interesting picture. One man at a corner table was hunched over a menu. Although his face was hidden in the shadows, Kelly recognized the stooped shoulders and bent back of Edgar Porter. A blond woman was sitting across from him.

"I wonder who that is over there with Mr. Porter?" Kelly said. "Do you suppose it's his wife?"

Aunt Alma looked across the room. "I don't think he's married. She's probably just a friend." She set her cup down. "Shall we go?"

They stood up and crossed the room toward the doorway. As they passed Edgar Porter's table, he glanced up from the menu.

"Hello, Mr. Porter," Aunt Alma said.

"Evening, Miss Maxwell," he responded gruffly. He looked at Kelly and narrowed his eyes in a way that made her shiver.

As they left Chowning's Tavern, Aunt Alma said thoughtfully, "The woman with Mr. Porter looked vaguely familiar. I feel as if I've seen her before." Then Aunt Alma shrugged. "I suppose I've seen her around town somewhere."

A strong breeze whipped up as they strolled down Duke of Gloucester Street. The twilight sky, which was darkening earlier than usual, was filled with heavy clouds. "Looks like we're going to get some rain tonight," Aunt Alma said, sighing. "Let's remember to set the pans out. If we get a heavy downpour, the roof is bound to leak again."

They quickened their steps as the sky blackened and the wind bent the trees that lined the street. Once inside the house, Aunt Alma switched on the small flashlight she carried in her purse and Jared lit two tall candles on the side table in the front hall. Aunt Alma aimed the flashlight into the cluttered living room. "I suppose I can't put it off much longer," she mumbled under her breath.

"What?" Jared asked.

"The yard sale. I've been hoping that some-where in the house I might find some really valu-able antiques that could be sold for a healthy price. But I'm afraid all the good pieces were sold years ago. All this," she said, gesturing with the flashlight, "is probably not worth much at all. Certainly, no-where near what I need to keep this house."

"We'll stay home tomorrow and help with the rest of the pricing," Kelly said quickly, then glanced at Jared, who nodded. She wanted to reassure Aunt Alma that the sale would be a success, but she wasn't so sure that was true.

Later, Kelly carried a candle down the black corridor. She set the candle on the dresser in her bedroom and began getting undressed. Outside, the wind slashed fiercely through the trees. Although it still had not yet begun to rain, Kelly put the large porcelain bowl on the floor beneath the spot where the ceiling had leaked a few days ago. A strong gust billowed the curtains and blew out the flickering candle flame. Kelly crossed the room and lowered the window.

In bed, she closed her eyes, but her mind was filled with too many confusing thoughts to fall asleep quickly: Aunt Alma's worry about being able to keep the house, the strange story of Elizabeth and the hidden gold coins, and the figure in blue that floated through the halls at night. Kelly tried to tell herself that she didn't really believe in ghosts. But what about the image in the camera obscura? And that soft rustling sound she and Aunt Alma had both heard out in the corridor?

She stared up at the ceiling, watching the shadow dance caused by the swaying tree limbs outside her window. Suddenly, she heard a soft swishing sound that seemed to be coming from out in the hallway. Kelly sat up, faced the door, and strained her ears. But all she heard was the rustling of leaves in the wind.

Just as Kelly sank back on the pillow, the ping of raindrops plunked against the windowpanes. Falling softly at first, after a few minutes, the drops escalated into a torrential downpour. Kelly listened for the inevitable plop of water falling into the porcelain bowl from the leaky ceiling. When the first drops hit the bowl, Kelly thought again of Aunt Alma's problem of raising enough money to make all the urgent repairs on the house she loved so much. Now, more than ever, Kelly wished she could do something to help her aunt.

She finally fell into an uneasy sleep, but awoke with a start after a short time. It was still raining, although the wind sounded less violent. A click, she thought, that's what woke me. Like a door closing. Kelly slipped out of bed and padded silently across the wooden floor. She stood for a second, ear to the door, then slowly opened it and peered into the gloomy hall. The air was filled with the scent of lilacs.

Somewhere, farther down the black corridor, she heard the same rustling sound she'd heard before. Feeling her way along the walls, Kelly followed the sound. When she reached the place where the narrow hall made a sharp turn into the central upper hall, she stopped and peeked around the corner.

Someone was slowly opening the attic door. Too late, Kelly remembered she hadn't locked it the last time she'd gone up there. Even in the dark, Kelly could see that it was a young woman wearing a long, full-skirted gown held out with hoops. Kelly held her breath when the young woman turned, appeared to look directly at her, and smiled slightly before turning and gliding slowly up the attic stairs.

Kelly crossed the floor, intending at first to follow the apparition up the stairs. Instead, she stood still, listening. But there was only silence.

Chapter 14

The sky was a brilliant blue the next morning and the sun streamed through the high curved windows. Leaves and twigs strewn around the yard were the only evidence of last night's storm.

Kelly had meant to rise early to help Aunt Alma with the yard sale pricing, but after last night's adventure, she had dropped into an exhausted, restless sleep filled with dreams of British soldiers and a blue-gowned Elizabeth roaming the halls hiding gold coins.

Kelly jumped out of bed, dressed quickly, and opened the windows. The air had a refreshing, just-washed feel and the temperature, for once, was surprisingly comfortable. As Kelly looked out at the magnolia trees still glistening with drops of water, she thought about seeing Elizabeth gliding up the attic stairs and about the disturbing dreams she had. Once again, she wondered if the British soldiers had ever found the gold coins. They *could* still be here somewhere, Kelly told herself stubbornly.

She whirled and strode across the room to the long dresser where she'd left the diary. Maybe there was some information, some clue in Elizabeth's diary that she'd missed.

That's funny, she thought, I'm sure it was on the dresser yesterday afternoon. The diary was gone. Had it been there when she went to bed last night? She couldn't be sure. It had been dark of course, with only the flickering candlelight. Could Jared have taken it to read? Or—

No. She couldn't believe Elizabeth had been in her room and taken it. But there had been that faint clicking sound of a door closing.

Kelly bolted from the room and ran down the long hallway. Jared and Aunt Alma were already at work in the living room. After apologizing for oversleeping, she got right to work, sorting small things into groups and putting stickers on pieces of furniture.

"Jared," she said, trying to sound casual, "did you happen to borrow Elizabeth's diary?"

"Nope," he said, grunting as he lifted a box of dishes to a spot near the doorway. He set the box down with a thud that made Aunt Alma jump. "Why?"

"Oh, I was just wondering. I . . . I guess I forgot where I put it." Aunt Alma frowned at her niece.

"I suppose you think your ghost took it," Jared muttered.

"I didn't say that," Kelly said quickly, glancing at Aunt Alma. Her aunt looked more tired than usual this morning, and Kelly didn't want to upset her with more talk of ghosts.

But it became apparent that Aunt Alma was already upset. She clung to the closest table to steady herself. "My room was filled with the scent of lilacs this morning," she said in a hushed voice, "and I dreamed there was somebody in my room during the night. At least, I thought it was a dream, but now . . . " Aunt Alma's face was drained of color and her hands shook.

Kelly and Jared exchanged worried looks. "Aunt Alma, I think you could use a cup of tea," Kelly said, taking her aunt's arm and gently guiding her toward the kitchen. "Jared can keep working on the pricing."

When she had Aunt Alma settled into a kitchen chair, Kelly put the teakettle on the stove and busied herself getting out cups and sugar.

"It's all just too much at once. Ghosts wandering around in the middle of the night . . . worrying about how to raise enough money to keep the house." Aunt Alma paused and smiled slightly.

"Ghosts and all. And Mr. Porter badgering me to sell him the house."

Kelly raised her eyebrows at that last statement.

"He was here again," Aunt Alma said in answer to Kelly's unspoken question. "Early this morning."

"Why should he be so anxious to buy this house anyway?" Kelly asked.

"Actually, he's mentioned tearing down the house and building a small apartment building on the land."

"That's terrible." Kelly put her hands on her hips. "Why, this house is historic. How can he even *think* of tearing it down?"

Aunt Alma looked at Kelly in surprise. "And to think, you were the young lady who insisted she had absolutely no interest in history."

Kelly blushed. "I guess I never knew how interesting history could be. Especially when it turns out that my very own ancestors were involved in secret Revolutionary plans and hiding gold coins."

"It is exciting, isn't it?" Aunt Alma sighed and said, almost to herself, "I certainly could use a few coins right now, gold or otherwise."

Kelly didn't say anything, but in the back of her mind, a plan began to form.

Chapter 15

Aunt Alma finally decided to hold the yard sale the following Saturday, then promptly went into a tizzy worrying about the weather. "I just hope it doesn't rain," she said for at least the tenth time.

Kelly smiled and said, "If it does, we can put a lot of things on the front porch and the larger pieces in the living room."

"Yes, of course," Aunt Alma agreed, bobbing her gray head.

But she needn't have worried. Saturday morning dawned clear and sunny, with not even a hint of rain in the air. After a hasty breakfast, Kelly and Jared began setting up tables for the sale items in the front yard. Chen arrived and helped them move chairs and tables from the living room onto the front porch.

They were still carrying boxes outside when the first customers arrived. Before long, the yard was crowded with people browsing through the items on the tables. Many of the low-priced things, such as brass flower bowls and ceramic knick-knacks, sold quickly.

"So, how's the big sale going, little girl?" Edgar Porter stood next to one of the tables.

Kelly straightened her shoulders. "It's going just fine, Mr. Porter." Why did he always call her "little girl"?

"This is a waste of time, you know," he said, looking at the articles piled on the long table.

Kelly didn't answer, but busied herself rear-ranging a pile of linens.

"Your aunt would be doing herself a favor to forget about trying to make money for repairs and just sell the house."

"Actually," Kelly said stiffly, "Aunt Alma will probably make more than enough to fix up the house."

Edgar Porter raised his bushy eyebrows. "Oh?"

"Yes," Kelly continued, "there are several very, uh, valuable antiques here."

"Is that so?" With that, Mr. Porter turned and strolled across the yard to where two faded brocade-covered wing chairs had been placed.

Business slowed down considerably around noon, with only half a dozen or so customers browsing among the tables and furniture. Aunt Alma carried out a platter of chicken salad sandwiches and a pitcher of lemonade. Kelly polished off her sandwiches quickly, then ran into the house to get her camera. It would be fun to have a few pictures of the yard sale to show her parents. When she came back outside, she saw that Mr. Porter was still hanging around. He was at the far end of the porch, closely examining the drawers of a walnut side table.

Why was he still here? Kelly wondered. She raised her camera and deliberately focused the telephoto lens on his profile. Quickly she adjusted the shutter speed to compensate for the shadows on the porch and snapped the picture. Kelly wasn't sure why she took the picture of Edgar Porter. There was just something odd about his behavior that made her curious to learn more about him.

Soon more people arrived. Kelly took her camera into the house, then hurried back to help with the sale. As she accepted money for a chair, she saw Edgar Porter standing at a nearby table talking to a young couple looking at a pair of pewter table lamps. Mr. Porter shook his head and gestured around the yard. After a few minutes, the couple set the lamps back on the table and headed for their car. Now, what was that all about? Kelly wondered.

A few minutes later, Jared stomped over to her. His face was flushed with anger as he whispered, "That peanut man is sabotaging our sale."

"What are you talking about?"

"I'll tell you what I'm talking about. I heard Mr. Porter tell that couple we're asking too much money for those lamps. He said most of the things are extremely overpriced and not worth buying."

"But, why would they even believe him?"

"Because he told them he was an antiques dealer and considered everything here worthless." Jared cracked his knuckles and scowled at Mr. Porter, who was now approaching a woman inspecting one of the Victorian sofas.

"Of all the nerve," Kelly said. "He *wants* this sale to be a flop. He probably thinks if the sale doesn't make much money, Aunt Alma will sell him this house." She grabbed her brother's arm. "Jared, we can't let him get away with this."

"No, we can't. Maybe I can do something about it." Jared marched across the yard.

After that, every time Mr. Porter started talking to a potential customer, Jared was at his side, touting the item in question. Finally, with a grim look, Edgar Porter left the yard and walked down the street without a backward glance.

Kelly ran over to Jared. "Mr. Porter didn't look

too happy when he left. What on earth did you say to him?"

"Nothing much. But at least as long as I hung around, he didn't have a chance to say anything derogatory about anything in the sale."

"Huh?"

"Derogatory—degrading, expressing a low opinion," Jared explained impatiently. He pulled off his glasses and blew on them. "You know something? I'm beginning to agree with you about that man. There's definitely something sneaky about him. When I heard him tell that one couple that he was an antiques dealer, well, that was news to me. So I asked him if he thought the Chippendale style was superior to the Bonweil style. And do you know what he said?"

Kelly shook her head in bewilderment. She knew nothing about furniture styles and had no idea what Jared was talking about.

"He said, and I quote," Jared emphasized, "'This piece of Bonweil has definitely got more style.'"

"So?"

"Oh, for Pete's sake, Kelly. There is no such furniture style as Bonweil."

"Oh." Kelly frowned, then suddenly understood what Jared meant. "Oh! So Edgar Porter doesn't know *anything* about antique furniture."

"Right. And that's not all. Remember Chen telling us Mr. Porter was retired from the navy?" Kelly nodded. Jared continued, "I asked him what rank he had when he retired." Jared paused dramatically before saying, "He told me he was a general."

"So?"

Jared thumped the side of his head with his hand. "Kelly, there are no generals in the navy. That's an *army* rank."

"But why would he lie about something like that?"

"Beats me. It doesn't make any sense."

"No," Kelly said. "And it doesn't make any sense that he told me he's interested in old houses, yet he told Aunt Alma he plans to tear this house down and put up an apartment building on the land. We'd better try to find out more about Mr. Edgar Porter. There's something weird going on around here."

Chapter 16

While they packed unsold items into cartons, Kelly thought about Edgar Porter. More than ever, she distrusted him. He was doing an awful lot of lying. And dumb lying at that. She didn't for a minute believe he was really interested in "charming" old houses or antiques. More than likely he planned to tear the house down and build an apartment building, as he had told Aunt Alma.

"Build an apartment!" Kelly nearly dropped the dish she was holding. Could the blueprints he was holding in that first picture she'd taken of Mr. Porter be drawings for an apartment building?

She carried a filled cardboard carton into the living room. Aunt Alma was sitting at a desk, counting money from the sale. "Well, we made enough to do some of the repair work," Aunt Alma said with a sigh. "But it's not nearly as much as I'd hoped for."

"You're not giving up are you? I mean, you're

not going to sell the house to Mr. Porter?"

Aunt Alma shook her head. "I honestly don't know *what* I'm going to do. I want very much to keep this house. Oh, I know it's far too big for me, but you see, I've been thinking. If I could only afford to fix it up, maybe I could rent out rooms to tourists or even to college students."

"That's a great idea," Kelly said.

"But it all comes back to the same thing. How will I pay for the repairs?" Aunt Alma stood up. "But don't you fret; that's *my* worry. Right now, I'm starving. Let's have dinner."

After dinner, Kelly wandered restlessly around the house. Although it was still light outside, the corridors and narrow twisting passages were dim and shadowy. She stopped in the upper central hall and studied the portrait of Elizabeth Harris. Jared might not believe that Elizabeth's spirit was still in the house where she grew up, but both Kelly and Aunt Alma had seen her. The guide in the Peyton Randolph House had said something about spirits and ghosts haunting places where tragedies had occurred. Had some tragedy taken place in this house? Something to do with Elizabeth?

A faint sound from behind the attic door across the hall caught Kelly's attention. She tiptoed across the pine floor, reached out, and cautiously curved her hand around the brass doorknob.

"Why are you going up to the attic?"

Kelly spun around. "Jared Brennan, I told you *never* to sneak up on me like that."

Jared shrugged. "You shouldn't be so jumpy. Why *are* you going up to the attic?"

"Oh, I thought I . . . I mean . . . uh . . . I want to see if I can find any more old letters. Maybe I can learn more about Elizabeth and her father's plan to help the patriots."

Jared narrowed his eyes and studied his sister. "Hmmn . . . Actually, I was looking for you. Chen and I are going to bike out the Country Road to Carter's Grove plantation tomorrow. You want to come along? Chen says we can rent bikes over at the Lodge."

"Sure, that sounds like fun. Aunt Alma said Carter's Grove is beautiful."

"We'll go first thing in the morning," Jared told her.

After Jared went downstairs, Kelly opened the attic door and climbed up the narrow staircase. She paused on the top step to look around the shadowy room. Walking across the floor, Kelly wondered if she had been silly to come up here. What she'd heard was probably only mice scurrying around.

Kelly picked up the camera obscura and stared

at the frosted glass for several minutes. This time, Elizabeth's image did not appear. Kelly sighed and set the old camera back down on the floor. Maybe the image *had* existed only in her imagination. She took a step toward the stairs, then stopped suddenly. Lying on top of a wooden trunk was Elizabeth's diary. She had forgotten it during all the activity involved with the yard sale.

But how did it get up here? Kelly picked up the small bound book and again looked around the room. The shadows were deepening now, and the far corners of the room were completely dark. The attic had the same musty, mildewy smell she remembered from a few days ago. But there was another smell, too. It was the faint scent of lilacs.

Chapter 17

The early morning air was cool. As Kelly pedaled along the Country Road with Jared and Chen, she was grateful for the break in the heat wave they'd been having. They rode slowly, enjoying the quiet of the woods and the fields. Tall, ramrod-straight loblolly pines towered over stands of mountain laurel on either side of the road. Soon, the road sloped downward and they pedaled over a curved causeway that spanned Tutter's Neck Creek. They paused on the causeway to watch a pair of mud turtles climb onto a log at the water's edge and Kelly took a few pictures.

The Country Road wound its way out of the woods, through open fields speckled with Queen Anne's lace, yarrow, and trumpet creeper, then plunged once more into deep, shaded forest.

As she rode along, Kelly's thoughts drifted to Elizabeth's diary. How *did* it end up in the attic? And what about the gold coins? They *could* still be somewhere in the house, she thought again. If only she could find them, then Aunt Alma wouldn't have to worry about being able to afford to fix up the house.

Kelly stopped pedaling suddenly. It occurred to her that while she kept *thinking* about how great it would be to find those old coins for Aunt Alma, she hadn't actually searched for them. OK, she told herself, it's time for some action. With a burst of energy, she pedaled faster to catch up with Jared and Chen. She would ask them to help her search for the coins. The house was so huge, it would be almost impossible to tackle this without help.

At Carter's Grove, they joined a group of people waiting to tour the mansion. Kelly used the waiting time to photograph the house and the grounds. The large brick house stood on high ground overlooking the James River. Tulip poplar trees stood proudly on the edge of the rise. Just below was a large garden planted with yellow squash, peas, butter beans, and an assortment of other vegetables.

"That's Wolstenholme Towne," Chen said, pointing down toward the river at a partially reconstructed wooden fort.

"That's the settlement that was destroyed in an Indian raid, isn't it?" Jared asked.

Chen nodded. "Back in 1622, more than a hundred years before this plantation was here. The settlement was never rebuilt. In fact, no one knew there had ever been a settlement down there until a few years ago, when archaeologists were doing some digging here."

Kelly snapped a picture of the fort. Smiling, she turned back toward the mansion.

"What are you smiling about?" Jared asked.

"Oh, I just had an interesting thought. I'll tell you about it later," she said mysteriously.

The door of the house opened just then, and there was no more time for questions as they climbed the steps and entered the eighteenth-century plantation house. It was huge, but unlike Aunt Alma's run-down house, this one had been restored and kept up beautifully over the years. The pine paneling in the spacious entrance hall shone with the rich, dark tones pine acquires after so many years.

Along with the rest of the group, they listened as a guide explained the differences between how various parts of the house were used in the eighteenth century and in this century. "Neither the east nor the west wings were part of the main house when it was built in the 1750s," the guide said. "Instead, the house stood with a kitchen building on one side and a laundry on the other. The 'hyphens' connecting the three buildings were not added until the early part of the present century."

Back outside, Kelly looked back at the mansion, trying to imagine it more than two hundred years ago, when the center section stood with a smaller building on either side.

"The house was a lot smaller then," Kelly said.

"But still big," Jare pointed out. "All the rooms in that original building are larger than rooms in homes built today."

For a moment Kelly thought about the things the guide had told them about the additions built onto the original structure. "It's a lot like Aunt Alma's house," she mused.

Jared gave a hoot. "Are you kidding? Aunt Alma's run-down old house is nothing like Carter's Grove."

"No, no. I'm not talking about appearances, or floor plans, or even the way it's been taken care of," Kelly said. She flung her arms around excitedly. "I'm talking about the fact that the center is the oldest part of the house. The side wings were added much later."

"Like two hundred years later. So?"

"Don't you see? Aunt Alma's house has had lots of additions over the years. But the center section is the oldest part, the original part of the house."

"That's probably true," Jared agreed. He looked at Chen, who only shrugged, then looked back at his sister. "Kelly, what are you getting at?"

"If you'll be quiet for a minute, I'll explain it to you." Kelly pointed across the lawn to a sprawling shade tree. "Let's go sit down over there."

After they wheeled their bicycles into the shade and were settled on the lush green grass, Kelly continued.

"OK. First of all, I know you don't agree, Jared, but I really think there's a chance those old gold coins could still be hidden in Aunt Alma's house." Kelly held up her hand before Jared could say anything. "The idea isn't as crazy as it sounds. After all, until a few years ago, nobody had any idea the settlement of Wolstenholme Towne was even on this property. If an *entire* settlement could be lost and forgotten for over three hundred years, why couldn't coins the Harrises hid a few hundred years ago still be right where the they put them?"

Jared gazed thoughtfully down toward the river where Wolstenholme Towne had once stood. "Well?" Kelly leaned forward anxiously. "What do you think?"

Chen's dark eyes sparkled and he smiled and nodded. "I guess it's possible."

"Possible," Jared agreed, "but not probable. Besides, Aunt Alma's house is huge. It would take forever to search every room thoroughly."

"You're right. The house *is* huge. But we don't have to search the *entire* house," Kelly cried. "We only have to search the center part—that's the only part that was built when Elizabeth and her family lived there!"

Jared jumped up suddenly. "I can't believe I'm saying this, but you're absolutely right. Smart thinking, Kelly."

Kelly grinned, absurdly pleased at the compliment. "I think it's worth a try," she said.

On the way back to town, Jared said thoughtfully, "The interior of the old part of the house might have been changed over the years. You know, walls taken down or added. The entire inside could have been rearranged."

"We can ask Aunt Alma. She'd at least know if anything's been changed in her lifetime."

Jared began pedaling fast and called over his shoulder, "Hurry up, Kelly. Do you want to look for gold coins or not?"

Chapter 18

They found Aunt Alma in the backyard weeding one of the many overgrown flower beds. Kelly told her about their plan to search the oldest part of the house. "Do you know if any changes have been made in that part of the house?"

Aunt Alma adjusted her wide-brimmed straw hat before answering. "No, I don't believe the original section of the house has ever been altered."

Jared nodded. "OK. Good. Let's start with the living room."

Kelly stood in the middle of the room. "If you were going to hide something valuable in this room, where would you put it?"

Jared didn't answer, but began walking slowly around the room, sliding his hands along the paneling that covered the walls. They spent the rest of the afternoon tapping walls and looking for sliding panels and loose floorboards.

"Maybe this was a silly idea after all," Jared

said after they'd made a thorough search of the four downstairs rooms.

"Let's not give up yet," Kelly said firmly. "There's still the second floor and the attic and cellar."

"Right. And maybe your friendly ghost will lead us to the gold," Jared teased.

"Did you really see a ghost?" Chen asked.

Kelly shrugged impatiently. "I've certainly seen something. And so has Aunt Alma."

"I'd like to see a real ghost," Chen said.

"Why don't you spend the night?" Jared suggested. "Maybe you'll get lucky. If you've got half the imagination my sister does, you can probably conjure up some sort of spirit."

Kelly scowled at her brother. "Just you wait, Jared. Maybe you'll find out there's more to this ghost than my imagination."

"Sure, sure. Come on, Chen, let's go check with Aunt Alma about you spending the night."

After the boys left the room, Kelly clenched her fists. "Jared thinks he's so smart," she muttered. An idea began to form in her mind, and she whirled around and charged up the stairs and down the narrow corridor to her bedroom. She got her camera bag and took out several rolls of film. At last she found the high-speed film she was looking for. Then she carefully wound the film into her camera and set the ISO dial to correspond with the film speed. She left the camera in her room, then went downstairs to help Aunt Alma.

Kelly busied herself getting out plates and silverware, all the while thinking about her plan. Soon Jared and Chen came into the kitchen, whispering and laughing.

"Now what are you two up to?" Aunt Alma asked.

"Nothing," Jared said quickly. He winked at Chen, who only ducked his head and grinned.

Kelly narrowed her eyes at the two boys. But she was too excited about her plan to worry about what they had been doing.

Later, back in her room, Kelly checked her camera equipment to make sure everything was ready. When she was sure Aunt Alma and the boys were settled in their rooms for the night, she tiptoed down the hall, her camera hung from the strap around her neck.

In the corner of the upper central hall, she crouched down beside the table. From that position there was a good view of the attic door as well as the doorways to both the north and south wing corridors. Although it was dark in the central hall, after a few minutes, Kelly's eyes adjusted to the dimness and she was able to see better than she'd expected to. She settled down to wait.

Eventually, Kelly's eyelids began to droop. She fought to stay awake, but lost the battle and soon dozed off. Suddenly she jerked awake, sensing that she was not alone in the hall. It took a moment for her eyes to readjust to the darkness, but she could make out movement near the attic door. She raised her camera, aimed it toward the door, and pressed the shutter.

Her knees and legs were cramped from remaining in the same position for so long, but Kelly held her breath, not daring to move. The now-familiar form, wearing a long, full gown, moved slowly across the main hall. Just as the figure reached the doorway leading to the south wing, Kelly snapped another picture.

Kelly's legs felt like rubber as she struggled to a standing position and tiptoed across the hall. The windowless south corridor was even darker than the main hall, and Kelly couldn't see a thing. But she heard the familiar rustling sound of the full skirt swishing down the hall and smelled the lingering scent of lilacs.

Suddenly, Kelly realized that the rustling was coming closer. She spun around and slipped back into the central hall. Flattening herself against the wall, she raised her camera, ready to snap another picture as soon as the figure rounded the corner. The ghost again crossed the central hall and this time moved toward the corridor that led to the tower wing. Camera poised, Kelly inched along the black hallway, following the sound of the rustling gown.

She heard a faint click, then the swish of skirts coming toward her. Feeling along the wall, she discovered an open doorway and slipped quickly into what she thought must be the small sitting room. From there she began snapping away in both directions with her camera, unable to tell whether she was taking pictures of an empty corridor or of Elizabeth.

After waiting a moment to be sure Elizabeth had gone past the sitting room, Kelly cautiously crept back into the hall and followed the wall until she came out into the main hall. From there she saw Elizabeth just as she opened the attic door and glided up the stairs.

Boy, Kelly thought excitedly, wait until Jared sees these pictures!

Chapter 19

Kelly woke early the next morning. She ran a brush through her curly hair, pulled on a pair of old navy shorts and an oversized red T-shirt with a picture of a poodle holding a camera, then hurried to her makeshift darkroom.

She watched anxiously while the first picture began to emerge in the chemical solution. It was the photo she'd snapped just as Elizabeth opened the attic door. Though slightly out of focus, the picture clearly looked like Elizabeth, with full blue gown and medium-length, wavy brown hair.

Kelly worked quickly, slipping each negative into the carrier of the enlarger, then sliding the developing paper into the various trays of chemicals. Some of the pictures, as she had expected, proved to be photographs of empty hallways. But as she peered into the solution to watch one of the prints develop, she gasped. The photograph showed Elizabeth coming toward her along the black corridor.

Her head was turned to one side and her long brown hair covered much of her profile. Behind her was another figure in a long blue gown, going in the opposite direction. As she hung the print to dry, Kelly studied it carefully.

Two ghosts? *Two* ghosts in blue gowns?

Kelly yanked open the heavy door of her darkroom and raced down the hall. She found Jared and Chen in the kitchen, eating cornflakes.

"Quick, upstairs. I've got to show you something."

"Oh, really?" Jared said between mouthfuls. "What are you so excited about?" He looked at Chen and grinned. "She wants to show us something. Wonder what it could be?"

"I have no idea," Chen said with a chuckle.

Kelly put her hands on her hips. "Go ahead, joke all you want. You won't be laughing after you see what I've got up in my darkroom."

"OK. Come on, Chen. We might as well see what my sister thinks is so exciting."

"Just look at this picture," she said when they entered the darkroom. "I used high-speed film so I wouldn't need a flash. This is the first shot I got. It was taken just as Elizabeth opened the attic door." She pointed out a few other pictures in which the figure was either partially hidden by doorways or else moving away from the camera. "And then," Kelly paused dramatically, "look at this one." She moved aside so Jared and Chen could see the photograph in which there were two figures in the dark hallway.

"Wha—" Chen's dark eyes widened. "Oh, my gosh." He grabbed Jared's arm. "Look!"

"I'm looking, I'm looking. But I don't believe it."

"So," Kelly said triumphantly, "it isn't just all my 'wild imagination.'"

"Uh . . . not so fast, Kelly," Jared said, taking his glasses off and wiping them on his T-shirt. "I . . . uh . . . think we have a slight problem here."

"Jared, maybe we better tell her," Chen said with a squeak in his voice.

Kelly looked first at Chen, then at her brother. "What? Tell me what?"

"Well," Chen said slowly, "it's about the ghost."

"What about it?" Kelly gestured impatiently toward her photographs. "You wanted scientific proof—I've got scientific proof."

Jared shook his head. "No, I'm afraid you don't."

"Jared," Kelly said in exasperation, "would you please tell me *what* you're talking about."

Jared took a deep breath. "The thing is, well,

I'm not surprised that you were able to get some pictures of a 'ghost.'"

"Wait a minute," Kelly said. "I thought you didn't believe in ghosts."

"I didn't. I still don't."

"And what, may I ask, are these?" Kelly waved her hands at the prints hanging to dry.

"Right. Uh . . . you see, I talked Chen into borrowing the dress his sister wears when she works in the Historic Area so he could dress up like the ghost of Elizabeth Harris and walk around the halls last night. He got the wig from a friend's mother."

"You did what!" Kelly's face went red with anger and her green eyes flashed.

"It . . . it was just a joke, Kelly," Chen said.

"Yeah, we just wanted to have a little fun," Jared added.

Kelly folded her arms across her chest and glared first at the two boys, then at the photographs, shaking her head in disgust. Then her eyes fell on the picture that showed two figures in long gowns. "Wait a minute," she said suddenly. "That explains *one* of the figures in this picture. But what about the *other* one?"

Jared shrugged and shook his head. "You got me there. I don't know who the other one is."

"It's Elizabeth's ghost, of course," Kelly said flatly.

"Not so fast, Kelly. From what I've read, ghosts, *if* they exist, can't be photographed. They're only a mass of energy, not flesh and bones. So if the second figure was a ghost or some sort of spirit, nothing would have shown up on your film, except possibly some sort of light area, an energy field. But *not* a recognizable picture like this."

"If this isn't a ghost of Elizabeth Harris, *who* is it?"

Jared again shook his head. "I have no idea. But you're right about one thing, Kelly. *Something* very strange is going on in this house."

Chapter 20

Aunt Alma called upstairs just as they left the dark-room. "I'm going to visit my friend over on North Boundary Street. We may do a little shopping, so I won't be home until midafternoon. Can you manage lunch on your own?"

"We'll be fine," Kelly assured her. "Have a nice time."

After Aunt Alma left, they went down to the kitchen and sat around the old oak table.

"I've been thinking," Kelly said. Jared rolled his eyes, but Kelly ignored him and continued, "You said it wouldn't have been possible to get a clear picture of a real ghost, right? So, if the second figure in the picture isn't a ghost, that means *somebody* else is *somehow* getting into this house and pretending to be the ghost of Elizabeth Harris."

Jared nodded. "But the question is *who* and *why?* Why would someone want us to think the house is haunted?"

Kelly shivered at the thought of a stranger dressed like a girl who had been dead for more than two hundred years coming into this house night after night and prowling the dark corridors. She glanced around nervously. "Let's go for a walk," she said. "Maybe we'll come up with some fresh ideas if we get out of here for a while."

"Good idea," Chen agreed, jumping up.

In the Historic Area they strolled down Palace green, where several sheep, tended by a young woman in colonial garb, were grazing. A Colonial Williamsburg guide, surrounded by a group of tourists, stood on the edge of the green.

Jared stopped suddenly. "What we need to do is think about this whole thing logically. Now, what facts do we know so far?"

"We know someone is coming into Aunt Alma's house."

"Right. But Aunt Alma always locks up at night and we've seen no evidence of any windows forced open."

"Maybe whoever it is has a key," Chen suggested.

"That's a possibility," Jared said.

"Suppose there's a secret entrance somewhere?" Kelly said. "After all, old houses sometimes have secret rooms and stuff."

"That's a little farfetched," Jared said. "But, I suppose we shouldn't rule it out until we've checked out the possibility."

"The attic," Kelly said. "Elizabeth, or whoever she is, always goes back up to the attic."

Jared frowned in concentration. "You may be onto something. Let's check out the attic more carefully. All we've ever really done up there is to look through all those old trunks."

They turned and hurried back down the green toward Duke of Gloucester Street. There Kelly saw the peanut shape of Edgar Porter at the edge of the green. As Kelly and the boys neared the wide street, Edgar Porter turned around. He frowned when he saw them, then hurried off down the street.

Kelly stared thoughtfully after him. Something was nagging at her. She felt as if there was something she was forgetting. Something that had to do with Edgar Porter.

Chapter 21

Back at Aunt Alma's house, they picked up flashlights from the kitchen, then tromped up the attic stairs. Outside, the sky was overcast and little light filtered through the dusty windows. Kelly beamed her flashlight around the large, cluttered space. Everything looked the same as it had the last time she'd come up there.

"Let's check the walls for loose boards or something," Jared suggested.

They moved methodically around the room, pressing on panels and tapping on the boards, listening for a hollow sound. It wasn't until they were inspecting the north wall that they found the closet. The door was in a far corner of the room and was only noticeable from very close to it.

"Why would anyone bother to build a closet in an attic?" Kelly wondered as she reached for the doorknob. She raised her eyebrows, then added, "Unless it's not really a closet."

"Hurry up," Chen said. "Open the door."

Kelly turned the knob and pulled the door toward her. She pointed her flashlight inside. The closet was very small and square shaped. And it was empty. "Oh," Kelly said with a sigh, "it *is* just a closet." She was about to turn away when Jared slipped past her and stepped inside the small enclosure.

With his flashlight on, he moved slowly around the walls, tapping on the wooden panels with his knuckle. "Hey, wait a minute." Jared set his flashlight down on the floor. "Shine your light over here," he told Kelly as he slid both his hands slowly up and down the panels. After a moment, there was a faint click. Jared pushed on the wall and the entire panel swung outward.

Kelly and Chen crowded into the closet, shining their flashlights into the opening. A narrow, twisting staircase led downward into complete blackness.

"A secret staircase," Kelly exclaimed. "Let's go down."

"Wait a minute," Jared cautioned. "The steps may be rotted. Let's go very slowly and test each step. I'll go first."

Kelly was annoyed that, as usual, Jared was taking charge. But she was too eager to see where the stairs led to make a fuss. They went down carefully, step by step. It was slow going, and for a while, it seemed as if there was no end in sight. The steps were steep and turned sharply several times.

At last Jared said, "We're almost to the bottom. I can see a room ahead."

They found themselves in a small, narrow room scarcely larger than an average bathroom. The floor was dirt and there were no windows or doors. The only furniture was a wooden chair in one corner.

Draped over the back of the chair was a long blue gown.

"That's it," Kelly cried. "That's what our ghost person wears."

"So, if someone gets into the house using that hidden stairway, then how do they get into and out of this little room?" Jared pointed out.

"Maybe there's another secret door," Chen said. Again they began pressing on the walls. But all four walls were brick, and not a single brick moved.

"There *has* to be a way out." Kelly frowned and flashed her light around the room again. "Let's go back up the stairs into the attic. Then we can get into the cellar from the front hall. Maybe there's a door opening from the other side of this wall."

They retraced their steps up the narrow stairway, moving more quickly now that they knew the steps were safe. Then back down the attic stairs they hurried and on down to the first floor. The sound of voices on the front porch brought them to a halt in the hallway.

"Well, Miss Maxwell," Edgar Porter was saying, "Have you made up your mind yet?"

"No, I haven't," Aunt Alma replied coldly.

Kelly tiptoed to the front door and peeked out.

"You couldn't have made enough money from your little yard sale to pay for all the work that's needed here," Mr. Porter said.

"That, Mr. Porter, is really none of your business."

"Now, don't get yourself all ruffled. What I think you should do is sell this old monstrosity and move into a cozy little apartment where you wouldn't have to worry about repairs and upkeep. After all, why hang on to such a huge place, living alone and all?"

"This house has been in my family for generations," Aunt Alma said.

"Ah, yes. So you've told me." Mr. Porter stood up. "Maybe it's time for a change, then."

Jared pushed past his sister and shoved open the screen door. "Mr. Porter, what kind of apartment building are you planning to build on this site?"

"Huh?" Mr. Porter narrowed his eyes, glared at Jared, then shrugged. "Oh, I'm still discussing things with my . . . uh . . . contractor."

"In that case, there's really no big hurry for me to make my decision is there?" Aunt Alma said.

"Letting this drag on could cost you, Miss Maxwell. I've offered you a fair price, but I can't guarantee that offer will hold for long." Mr. Porter turned abruptly and stomped down the porch steps.

Jared watched him head down the street. "For a man in real estate development, Mr. Porter doesn't know much about today's economy."

"Whatever do you mean, dear?" Aunt Alma asked.

"The other day at the yard sale, I casually mentioned that I'd heard on the news that interest rates were climbing. You know, just making polite conversation with him."

"And?" Kelly asked. Why couldn't her brother ever get to the point quickly?

"And Mr. Porter said, 'Really? I hadn't heard.' Dad's friend in real estate is always talking about interest rates. It's essential to keep track of data like that if you're into buying and selling property."

Aunt Alma nodded. "I'm beginning to not quite trust that man. I'm not sure why, but I have this odd feeling about him."

Chapter 22

They decided to forget about Mr. Porter and headed for the cellar. "You know, we still haven't searched the cellar for the gold coins," Kelly said. "A gloomy old cellar might be a good hiding place."

"Maybe," Jared said. "But right now we need to find a way into that little room at the bottom of the secret staircase."

They had never been down in the cellar before, but they weren't surprised to find it had never been wired for electricity. Slashes of light came through two windows set high on one wall that faced the backyard. But it was barely enough to dispel the gloomy, damp atmosphere.

The cellar was divided into three small rooms and one large one with an oversized fireplace taking up an entire wall.

With brow wrinkled in concentration, Jared crossed the large room to the fireplace. "From everything I've read and heard, the kitchen in an eighteenth-century Williamsburg house was always a separate building away from the main house. It was more practical that way because there was the problem of heat and smoke during the hot summers. Also, kitchen fires were pretty common. But this sure looks like a cooking hearth. I wonder why the Harrises had their kitchen down here instead of in a separate building?"

Kelly shrugged impatiently. "Who cares. Let's look for a hidden door."

On the assumption that the tiny hidden room was behind the east wall of one of the smaller rooms, each took a different section of the wall and began pushing at the bricks. They worked silently for several minutes, only to find that this side of the wall was just as solid as the other side.

"It's no use," Kelly said at last. "This wall won't budge." She twisted a strand of hair and muttered to herself, "But there *has* to be a way into that little room."

A scurrying sound in one corner of the dank room made Kelly jump. "It's just a mouse," Jared told her, grinning.

"I knew that." Kelly turned and marched out into the larger room. The light from her flashlight showed a few old wooden barrels, a big, black potbellied stove, some rusted shovels and hoes, but little else except a lot of cobwebs. "No one seems to have bothered with this cellar for years. I think we ought to thoroughly search these rooms for the gold coins."

"Kelly, let's concentrate on one thing at a time. Forget the coins for now." Jared pushed back the clump of hair that always fell over his forehead. "I mean, for Pete's sake, *someone* is getting into this house and wandering around in eighteenth-century clothes. I think we should find out who's doing it and why."

Kelly knew her brother was right, but she was still anxious to look for the coins. Finding them might help Aunt Alma decide not to sell the house to that pushy Mr. Porter.

"Mr. Porter!" she exclaimed.

"Huh? What about him?"

"He's so obviously in a big hurry to buy this place. Why? Could he know there are valuable gold coins hidden somewhere in the house?"

"But how would he know about them? *We* don't even know if they're still here," Jared pointed out.

"I don't know *how* he would know about them," Kelly said with a trace of impatience. "But just suppose he does know there might be gold hidden here. That would explain why he's so anxious and in such a big hurry to buy the house. He wouldn't want to take a chance on Aunt Alma coming across the coins." Kelly paused to catch her breath. "Maybe *he's* dressing up like Elizabeth and pretending to be a ghost to frighten Aunt Alma into selling the house."

"One thing wrong with that, Kelly. That picture you took of what you thought were two ghosts."

"What about it?" she demanded.

"As I recall, the two ghosts in the picture were about the same height."

"So? Jared, will you just tell me *what* you are getting at?"

"So, Mr. Porter is quite a bit taller than Chen."

Chen nodded. "Jared's right, Kelly."

"Let's go have another look at those pictures," Kelly said. She ran up the cellar stairs ahead of Jared and Chen.

A few minutes later, they stood in Kelly's darkroom, studying the photographs. Kelly had to admit that, once again, her younger brother was right. The two figures *were* about the same height. Unfortunately, both faces were turned away from the camera and it was impossible to identify either from their figure alone.

"Well, there's only one thing to do," Jared said. "Take more pictures of our ghost."

Chapter 23

That night Kelly and Jared worked quickly setting up the tripod and camera in the main upstairs hall. Kelly carefully focused the lens on the attic door while Jared stretched the cable release over a chair, letting it dangle over the edge where he could crouch out of sight and operate it.

"It's all set," Kelly whispered. "This camera has an automatic advance, so all you have to do is keep pressing the bulb." She tiptoed back down the hall to her bedroom and picked up her other camera, then left the door partially open and sat on her bed to wait.

After what seemed like hours, Kelly heard a slight rustling sound out in the hall. She crept over to the door and peered into the hallway just as someone turned and headed back in her direction. Kelly lifted her camera and snapped the shutter button, then ducked back into her room to wait until the "ghost" passed her doorway.

When she could tell the rustling sound was moving away from her, she slipped back out into the hall and at a safe distance made her way down the black corridor. At the turn into the central hall, she leaned around the corner and snapped several more pictures before the figure disappeared up the attic steps.

The next morning, after a quick breakfast of pancakes and blueberry syrup, Kelly hurried up to her darkroom. She forced herself not to work too quickly. She didn't want to spoil any of the pictures she and Jared had taken during the night. As she watched each image appear on the paper, she was pleased to see that, this time, there were several photographs in which the mysterious figure in blue was facing the camera.

She lifted the last photograph out of the rinsing tray, hung it up to dry with the others, and switched on the overhead light to study each print. The face of the woman in the photograph looked vaguely familiar, but Kelly could not remember when she had seen this person before.

Kelly cleaned up her work area, putting the chemicals away and washing trays and tongs, then went to find Jared. He was outside, pruning holly bushes, but stopped when he saw his sister. "Well? How did the pictures turn out?"

Kelly told him about the prints and her feeling that she had seen the woman before. "Come on," she said. "I'll show you."

Upstairs in Kelly's darkroom, Jared studied the pictures for several minutes without speaking. "The hair is wrong, of course," he finally said. "But it's probably a wig."

Kelly peered closely at the photograph Jared pointed to. Suddenly, her green eyes widened in recognition. "It's the woman we saw in Chowning's Tavern with Edgar Porter! But why is she dressing up and pretending to be a ghost?"

"I don't know, but I'm beginning to think you're right, Kelly. Mr. Porter *does* have something to do with this ghost business."

"Let's show these pictures to Aunt Alma," Kelly suggested, taking the prints that were already dry off the line.

They found Aunt Alma in the kitchen, removing a tray of gingerbread cookies from the oven. The tangy smell of cinnamon and cloves filled the air. "These will be cool enough to eat in just a few minutes," Aunt Alma told them. "I'm going to send a platter over to Chen to thank him for helping with the yard sale."

"They smell wonderful, Aunt Alma. But sit down. We have something to show you." Kelly told her about taking pictures of the "ghost" the other night and again last night, and Jared explained why they believed the figure was not a ghost after all, but a real-live person.

"My goodness," Aunt Alma said. "I did hear that rustling sound last night, but I was too nervous to come out of my room." She frowned. "Actually, I think I'd have been even more uneasy knowing the ghost was a real person and not some spirit. No, come to think of it," she added, "the idea of some stranger secretly coming into my house and wandering about makes me just plain angry!"

"I understand how you feel," Kelly said. "Here, look at these pictures."

Aunt Alma squinted closely at the photograph Kelly handed her. "So, this is the ghost?"

"And it's the woman we saw with Mr. Porter at Chowning's," Jared explained. "She's wearing a brown wig or else she's dyed her hair. She had blond hair when we saw her at the tavern."

"You know, that evening in Chowning's, I thought she looked familiar. She reminds me of somebody. But I couldn't imagine who. I still can't."

Kelly nibbled on one of the cooled gingerbread cookies. "Well, now we know who our 'ghost' is—sort of. So, what do we do? Ask Mr. Porter who his friend is and why she's been haunting this house?"

Jared shook his head. "Of course not. Mr. Porter would probably just deny it or lie to us. Let's not tip our hand. If he knows we suspect anything, we'll never find out what's going on."

Kelly sighed and reached for another cookie. "I guess you're right. And we still don't know how she gets in and out of the little room next to the cellar."

Jared cracked his knuckles. "Right. Let's go have another look down there. There has to be some way into that little room besides from the attic."

Lighting their way down the stairs with flashlights, Kelly mused, "Why would someone build a hidden staircase in this house anyway? What do you suppose this tiny room was used for?"

"I bet it was part of the Underground Railroad," Jared said.

"Huh?"

"Kelly, don't you remember anything you studied in history? The Underground Railroad was a system devised to help slaves from southern states escape to the North during the 1800s. Whoever lived here at that time was probably involved in hiding and helping slaves."

"Oh."

Once again they checked the brick walls, and once again they found no hidden door.

Finally, Kelly threw up her hands in disgust. "I give up. Maybe she really is a ghost. It looks as if she simply vanishes into thin air. There is *no* way out of here."

"Kelly, don't go getting goofy on me now. You know she's not a ghost. She's a real person."

"Wait a minute," Kelly cried suddenly. "We haven't checked the wall outside."

"Now, *that's* a good idea," Jared said approvingly.

In the backyard where tall, tangled boxwood and holly grew along the rear wall of the house, Jared dropped to his knees and searched under the greenery.

"I think I see something," he exclaimed. He wriggled his body beneath a small opening in the leafy growth and was out of sight when Kelly heard a thud and a squeak. "Here it is!"

Kelly jumped up and down. "All right! We found it, we found it!"

A minute later, Jared backed out, still on his hands and knees. "There's a small wooden door behind the bushes. It has a metal ring that pushes it inward into a narrow passage. I had to crawl into the passage. There isn't enough head space to stand up." Jared grinned. "Come on. Let's make our plans. We're going to catch our mysterious ghost."

Chapter 24

A nd just how are we going to do that?" Kelly demanded.

"I have an idea, but the details need working out. Come on, let's take those cookies over to Chen. I'm sure he'll want to be in on this."

Minutes later, Kelly and Jared were seated on Chen's front steps, munching gingerbread cookies while Jared explained his plan.

"OK, Kelly, tonight you dress up in the blue gown and the brown wig that Chen wore the other night. Then you wait in the upper hall until this woman comes down from the attic."

"What if she doesn't show up tonight? What am I supposed to do, sit in the hall all night?"

"The point is, I think she *will* show up. Mr. Porter has been around, so I think he's getting impatient for Aunt Alma to make her decision to sell him the house. And if he wants to buy it because he thinks there may be old gold coins hidden here, it means he probably doesn't know exactly *where* they're hidden."

"Wait a minute," Kelly interrupted. "What makes you think he doesn't know where the coins are?"

"Well, think about it, Kelly. If he knew for sure where the coins were hidden, he wouldn't have to buy the house. He wouldn't have to go to all this trouble to make Aunt Alma think the house is haunted. He'd just find a way to steal them!"

"Right," Chen agreed. "He could just sneak in the secret doorway in through the cellar and steal the coins."

Kelly scowled. Why hadn't she thought of that? "All right. So, I dress up like Elizabeth and wait in the hall. Then what?"

Jared leaned forward. "Here's what you do."

That evening after dinner, Kelly, Jared, and Chen shut themselves into Jared's room. Kelly and the boys worked out what she was supposed to say and do when the woman came down from the attic, then Kelly practiced until they were all satisfied. She didn't know if the hard knots in her stomach were due to excitement or nerves. Probably both, she decided.

Finally, it was time for Kelly to slip into the

long, full-skirted blue gown. Although her hair was the same chestnut brown as Elizabeth's in the portrait, Kelly's was quite a bit shorter. She pulled the wig on over her own hair and made sure it was firmly in place, then stood back to look at herself in the full-length mirror.

"You really do look a lot like Elizabeth Harris," Jared told her. "Maybe you should let your hair grow. It, uh, looks nice like that."

Kelly blushed. A compliment from her brother was almost unheard of.

"You look great, Kelly," Chen chimed in.

Kelly grinned. "I just hope I don't trip over this dress. I'm not used to wearing long skirts."

"OK," Jared said. "Time to take our places. Ready?"

No moon lent its silvery light to the black night and the corridors were completely dark. Kelly positioned herself in a chair in an inky corner of the main upper hall, prepared for what might be a long wait. Jared and Chen waited just around the corner in the south corridor. A short time later, almost as if on cue, there was a faint click. Kelly's heart began to pound as the attic door swung open.

Chapter 25

K elly rose and walked slowly across the hall toward the attic door.

"You cannot have my gold coins," Kelly said in a low, whispery voice.

The woman let out a yelp and whirled around. It was too dark to see her face clearly, but Kelly could see movement as the woman backed up until she bumped into the wall.

"You cannot have my gold coins," Kelly repeated.

"Who . . . who are you?" the woman whispered.

"I am Elizabeth Harris. I know all about you and your friend, Edgar Porter." Kelly took a step toward her. "You think you will find my coins. But you will *never* find them."

"Of course we will," the woman snapped, then stopped in confusion. Suddenly, she whirled around, shoved past Kelly, and yanked open the door to the attic.

Just then, someone dashed past Kelly and clattered down the hall stairs. A voice hissed, "Follow her, Kelly."

For a moment, Kelly couldn't decide what she should do. Then, she gathered up her long skirt and raced up the attic stairs after the "ghost" woman. Past crates and around trunks, she made her way across the attic floor to the closet.

Just as she yanked open the door, Aunt Alma called from below, "Whatever is going on up there?"

Kelly did not bother to answer, but started down the twisting stairway. She felt as though she were descending into a black well. It was hard to move quickly when she could not see, and she wished desperately for a flashlight. Then she heard the woman's footsteps below. She must be about halfway to the bottom, Kelly thought.

Suddenly, Kelly stopped. There was a flash of light, then footsteps coming back *up* the stairs. Good grief, Kelly thought, why on earth is she coming back this way? Bewildered, Kelly, too, turned and headed back up the staircase. She reached the attic closet and slipped through the panel door, then out into the attic.

Seconds later, the ghost woman stepped out, followed by Jared and Chen, waving flashlights and panting.

"Are you people crazy?" the woman sputtered.

"I think . . . you owe us . . . an explanation," Jared gasped, struggling to catch his breath.

After a moment's pause to catch her own breath, the woman said icily, "I don't have to explain anything to a bunch of kids."

"Ah, but you do have to explain to me, since *you* are obviously trespassing in *my* house," Aunt Alma said from the top of the attic steps.

Aunt Alma led the way down to the kitchen, where they all sat down around the oak table. The woman looked first at Aunt Alma, then at Kelly and Jared and Chen. Then putting her hands over her face, she sobbed quietly.

"Edgar said it would be easy. All I had to do was dress up like the girl in that old portrait and wander around pretending to be her ghost." She paused and pulled off the brown wig. "He said I would only have to come here a few times. He was sure you'd be so scared you'd be more than willing to sell him the house. But then—"

"But then he found I wasn't giving in so easily. All right," Aunt Alma said with a sigh, "so we know now that you and Mr. Porter are in this together. What I want to know is *why* he's so anxious to buy this old house."

The woman glanced uneasily at Kelly before

speaking. "Uh . . . because of the gold coins."

"Gold coins!" Aunt Alma shook her head. "Young lady, that is ridiculous. That story about hidden gold is just that—an old story. No one knows what happened to the coins or if they ever existed in the first place."

"That's not what Edgar says. He thinks they're still here somewhere."

"Say," Jared asked, "how did Mr. Porter know about the coins anyway?"

"When Edgar was a teenager, he used to do odd jobs for Miss Maxwell's grandfather. The old man used to tell him all these weird stories about this house and his ancestors. Edgar claims he didn't believe most of them, but the story about the gold coins stuck in his mind."

"And I suppose Mr. Porter saw Elizabeth's portrait and discovered the hidden door behind the bushes when he was working here, too," Jared said.

The woman nodded. "He never told anybody about the secret entrance. I don't think even your grandfather knew it was there."

Aunt Alma had been frowning while she listened to the young woman. "I feel as though I've seen you before."

"My name is Nadine Wexford." She tossed her

head and sat up straighter. "Maybe you knew my mother. I'm told I resemble her."

Aunt Alma raised her eyebrows. "Your mother?"

"Jane Maxwell."

Aunt Alma stared thoughtfully at the woman, then nodded. "Of course. Cousin Jane. She looked very much like you when she ran off to California with that man. She was only sixteen, if I recall correctly."

"Yes. She and Arthur were married, and I was born a few years later. My parents died in an accident about three years ago. But my mother did tell me all about her grandfather and his wonderful old house."

Aunt Alma ran her hand through her hair. "This is all so confusing."

Kelly had been listening quietly to the exchange between Nadine and Aunt Alma, but now she jumped up and began pacing the room. "Wait a minute, this means you're Aunt Alma's second cousin. If you are, how come she never even knew you existed until now?"

Nadine shrugged. "Mother was so bitter about her family that she didn't want any part of her relatives. She never told them about me. But she always believed this house should be mine someday.

Things hadn't been going too well for me in California, so I decided to come back east and look up the family."

"But you didn't do that. Instead you snuck into this house and tried to scare Aunt Alma. Why?" Jared demanded.

Nadine stared down at the tabletop. "Everything went wrong. The day I arrived in town, I read in the newspaper about Great-uncle Edward's death and then learned that his niece Alma Maxwell had inherited this house and everything in it." Nadine clenched her fists on top of the table. "Mother always said *she* was Uncle Edward's favorite niece. She always expected him to leave the house to her and any children she had."

Aunt Alma cleared her throat and said, "Well, now—"

But Kelly cut in, "You've explained how you ended up here in Williamsburg. What I'd like to know is how Edgar Porter fits into all this."

"Yes," Aunt Alma agreed. She stood up, adding, "I'm going to put on some water for tea. Nadine, I think you still have a lot more explaining to do."

Chapter 26

No one spoke until Aunt Alma had filled the teakettle and Kelly set cups and saucers on the table. Chen's dark eyes darted from one person to another as he listened to all the questions and answers. His only comment was an occasional "Wow."

Now Jared took off his glasses, cleaned them with a napkin, and said to Nadine, "How do you happen to know Edgar Porter?"

Nadine stared into her teacup as if expecting to find an answer in the pale amber liquid. "Actually, we met quite by accident." She explained that one day soon after her arrival in Williamsburg, she had decided to go to see the house that had once meant so much to her mother. She had been standing in front of the house when a man came by. "He asked me if I knew the owner and mentioned that he had done some work there when he was young. One thing led to another and . . . " Her voice trailed off and she looked helplessly at Aunt Alma. "I should never have let Edgar talk me into his crazy scheme. It sounded like a good idea at first. But, after I'd come here a couple of times, I told him I didn't want to be involved in his plan." Nadine dropped her head and again began to sob. "Edgar said it was too late to back out."

Aunt Alma stood up. "Well, one good thing has come out of this. I have made a definite decision about this house." She glanced out the kitchen window and nodded to herself. "It's nearly dawn. As soon as it's light, I intend to call Mr. Porter and invite him to come over."

A couple of hours later when there was a knock at the front door, Kelly jumped up and ran from the kitchen to the front hall. "Good morning, Mr. Porter," she said coolly as she opened the door to him.

"Morning, little girl." Edgar Porter peered into the dim hall behind Kelly. "Your aunt called and asked me to come over."

"She's in the kitchen. Please follow me."

"Morning, Miss Maxwell," Mr. Porter said as he stepped into the large, sunny room. He smiled broadly and added, "So, you've finally decided to sell."

"Sit down, Mr. Porter," Aunt Alma told him,

her voice dripping icicles. "I have no intention of selling this house to you."

"I thought . . . I mean, when you phoned me so early in the morning, naturally I assumed—"

"Your plan to frighten Aunt Alma into selling you her house didn't work, Mr. Porter," Kelly said.

Edgar Porter's dark eyes narrowed. "I don't know what you're talking about," he said flatly.

"It's over, Edgar."

Mr. Porter twisted around in his chair so quickly, Kelly thought his neck would snap.

Nadine stepped into the kitchen and said again, "It's all over. Finished. They know the whole story."

Mr. Porter leaped up and his chair toppled over, crashing to the floor. "Na . . . Nadine. What are you doing here?"

Nadine shrugged. "These kids were a lot smarter than we were, Edgar."

Chapter 27

A few days later, Kelly and Jared sat on the front porch. It was yet another hot, hazy, and humid day in Williamsburg. Kelly fanned herself with a magazine and mentally reviewed the excitement of the past days. She was certainly going to have a lot to tell her parents.

Jared grinned at his sister. "Boy, Kelly, you sure had Edgar Porter pegged from the beginning when you said there was something strange about him. Can you believe he didn't want his picture taken because he'd deserted from the navy years ago and was still afraid the authorities might somehow see the picture and trace him!"

"And now, he's in trouble anyway. Aunt Alma filed a complaint against him for trespassing. I'm glad Aunt Alma's not selling her house to him." Kelly tugged on a strand of hair. "I feel a little sorry for Nadine, though. I have a feeling Aunt Alma does too. After all, they *are* related."

Jared nodded. "I wouldn't be surprised if Aunt Alma and Nadine manage to heal the troubles between them."

"But catching the ghost didn't really solve Aunt Alma's problems. She's still not sure how she can afford to keep the house." Kelly absently watched a yellow butterfly flit around the boxwood, then said, "Jared, suppose Mr. Porter is right about the coins? They could still be here somewhere."

Jared cracked his knuckles and wrinkled his forehead. "It's a long shot, but with all the other crazy things that have been going on . . . No, we'd probably be wasting our time."

But Kelly jumped up, her green eyes shining. "Come on. It won't hurt to have one more look. Besides, we never did search the cellar."

So, armed with flashlights, they went into the cellar once more. Light from Kelly's flashlight flicked around the large main room, while she pondered where to begin. "What about the floor?" she said at last. "It's part brick and part dirt. The coins could have been buried in the floor."

"Maybe," Jared agreed. "But we'd have to dig up the whole cellar."

Kelly laughed. "I never said it would be easy. At least it's cooler down here."

They found a couple of rusted shovels in one

corner and began digging. It was very slow, hard going. The dirt was firmly packed, and in most places it was almost impossible to break through the rock-hard soil.

After an hour of poking and digging, Jared slumped down on a crate. "This is crazy."

"Come on, Jared, you agreed to help. We can't give up now."

"Why not?" Jared asked.

"Because we just can't, that's why," Kelly told him, slightly breathless from her efforts. Beads of perspiration trickled down her face, despite the cellar's considerably cooler temperature. In frustration she jumped on the scoop of the shovel in an effort to force it through the hard floor surface.

"Hey!" she cried. "I've struck something."

Jared hopped off the crate and aimed the flashlight down at where Kelly was digging.

"It feels like metal, maybe a box or chest or something."

Jared fell to work with his shovel. After several minutes of hard work, they managed to uncover the tip of a piece of corroded metal. With triumphant looks at each other, they continued digging furiously.

"Stop a minute," Jared said. He knelt and began rocking the object back and forth to pry it loose. "Here, grab hold."

Finally, under their combined efforts, the earth gave way and they both fell sideways as they yanked the object free.

Kelly sat up and stared at what they had pulled out of the ground.

"It's only an old cooking pot," Jared said quietly. "I've seen some like this over in the Historic Area."

Kelly picked up the kettle and studied it for a moment, then tossed it aside in frustration. She wrapped her arms around her knees and sighed.

"Kelly, I know you'd like to find those gold coins. But I think it's hopeless. They were probably discovered years ago. For all we know, the British soldiers found them when they came back to search the house."

"I know, I know. But, Jared, don't you want to help Aunt Alma keep the house?"

"Sure I do. I just don't think all this digging is getting us anywhere."

Kelly's arms ached. Although she had no intention of giving up so easily, she did agree to stop for a break.

After gulping down a glass of cold apple juice, Kelly climbed the stairs to her bedroom and curled up on the window seat. The coins are still here somewhere, she told herself. They just *have* to be. Kelly sighed. But where? Then she jumped up and ran down the hall to the attic door. Maybe there was some clue in Elizabeth's diary, something she had overlooked.

She found the diary on top of one of the trunks. The camera obscura still lay on the floor where she'd left it. Funny, in all the excitement of the ghost, she'd actually forgotten about the camera obscura and the image she'd seen on the glass.

Kelly stooped and examined the glass closely. "Elizabeth, did I really see your image or was it just my imagination?" Kelly waited, half hoping to see the image again. For a fleeting second, she thought she did see something, but then the glass was blank. Kelly stood up, shaking her head. "Maybe I *do* have too much imagination," she mumbled.

Back in her room, Kelly again curled up on the window seat and opened the diary. She turned the fragile pages carefully until she came to the first entry that mentioned the gold coins. Again she read Elizabeth's description of the British soldiers' visit and again thought about how frightened Elizabeth must have been. Elizabeth died the day after she last wrote in her diary. Did that mean the soldiers were responsible for her death? Or had something else happened? She could have died from any number of causes. She could have even slipped in a muddy street and been trampled by a runaway horse.

Elizabeth wrote that the gold was "well hidden in the very depths of darkness." *Had* the British soldiers found the gold? Kelly closed the diary with a sigh. There were so many questions to which she would never know the answers.

She looked out the tall window into the backyard. Now that Jared had mowed the tall, weedy grass, it was possible to see the low brick rubble of the foundation of what Aunt Alma told them was once the eighteenth-century kitchen building. At one end, the low remains of a chimney protruded above the foundation.

Kelly stared thoughtfully at the remains for a few minutes, then ran out of the room and down the hall.

Chapter 28

S he found Jared and Aunt Alma in the kitchen making grilled cheese sandwiches for lunch. "Aunt Alma," she said breathlessly, "do you know when the old kitchen building was built?"

Aunt Alma raised her eyebrows. "Not precisely. Grandfather said it was probably constructed around the middle of the eighteenth century. Why do you ask?"

Kelly tugged on a strand of hair and didn't answer immediately.

Jared poured milk into tall glasses. "OK, Kelly," he said. "Out with it."

"I was just thinking." She paused to glance quickly at her brother, but for once he didn't roll his eyes, so she continued, "The separate kitchen building must have used for cooking when Elizabeth lived here. And that means that big fireplace down in the cellar was probably no longer used at all." Kelly's eyes were bright with excitement.

"Hmmn," Jared murmured. Then he winked at Kelly and said, "Eat first, then we'll talk."

Aunt Alma looked at her niece and nephew in confusion, opened her mouth to speak, then abruptly closed it again.

Kelly downed two grilled cheese sandwiches in record time and chugged her glass of milk. "Hurry up, Jared."

Back down in the cellar, they peered by the light of both their flashlights around the large fireplace at the end of the main room.

Kelly got down on her hands and knees and crawled into the open hearth. She pointed the beam of light up the chimney, moving the light slowly up and down. "Nothing," she muttered, backing out of the wide opening. "Let's check for loose bricks. Maybe there's a hollow space behind them."

Then, "That's funny," Kelly said. "Why would anyone put bricks in this strange pattern?" The circle of light disclosed a semicircular patterned area about eighteen inches high and two feet wide.

"That was probably a bake oven," Jared said. "Remember, we've seen those in a couple of the historic kitchens. They used them to bake bread and rolls and stuff."

"But why is this one bricked over?"

Jared shrugged. "After this room stopped being used as a kitchen, there'd be no need for a bake oven, obviously."

"But then why not brick over the large fireplace opening, too."

"Maybe nobody ever got around to finishing the job."

"Oh." But, although that sounded like a reasonable explanation, something about the bricked-over oven bothered her. "The depths of darkness," Kelly said softly. "Elizabeth wrote that the coins were hidden 'in the very depths of darkness.'"

Jared ignored her mumbling and continued to look for loose bricks on the fireplace front.

Suddenly, Kelly knew what was bothering her. "Jared, why would anyone go to the trouble of bricking over the oven and fireplace at all? Why bother closing it off? Unless—unless there was some reason to cover up the opening!"

Jared stared at his sister. "Oh, my gosh. You might be right."

None of the bricks covering the bake oven would budge. Jared scrounged around the cellar until he found a pick, and then they took turns chipping away at the crumbling mortar and brick. It was slow, dusty work, but they were too excited to notice or care how dirty and tired they were getting. They finally managed to pry loose several bricks, and Kelly poked the flashlight into the black hole.

"I see something!" she shouted.

Working as quickly as they could, they managed to free several more bricks and enlarge the opening. Jared slid the pick into the hole while Kelly pointed the beam of light inside. Inch by inch, using the point of the pick, he pulled an object toward the opening.

"I can hardly move it," Jared grunted. "It's some sort of box, and it's really heavy."

At last, Jared maneuvered the box close enough to touch. It took both of them to lift the metal box down to the floor.

"Oh, Jared," Kelly whispered. "Do you think this is it? You open it. I'm too nervous."

Jared shook his head. "Nope. You do the honors. After all," he said with a grin, "this was your idea."

It took Kelly a few minutes to pry loose the jammed lid. She lifted the lid slowly while Jared held the flashlight.

The chest was filled with gold coins.

Chapter 29

L ate that afternoon, Kelly and Jared sat on the front porch steps, sipping lemonade and munching spicy oatmeal cookies.

Aunt Alma sat in her favorite white wicker chair. Her eyes were bright and she kept running her plump hand through her hair, saying over and over, "I can't believe it. I just can't believe it."

Chen was there, too. Jared had just finished telling him about finding the coins.

"Wow," Chen said. "Do you two always have this much excitement when you go on vacation?"

Kelly laughed. "Actually, I expected this to be a pretty boring summer." She glanced quickly at her aunt and added, "I mean, because Dad wanted me to learn history and all."

Aunt Alma just smiled and nodded. "Thanks to you two, I can make all the repairs on the house and carry out my plan to rent a few rooms."

Kelly glanced sideways at her brother. "Your

plan to catch the ghost was a good one."

"But I probably would have never gotten the idea if not for the pictures you took," he admitted. "And we would never have found the coins if you hadn't refused to give up."

Kelly grinned at her brother. Guess we're *both* smart about different things, she thought. Jared returned her grin.